## Garfield's Apprentices book 2

Leon Garfield has made a particular name for himself
as a writer of stories for childern set in the eighteenth
century. He has been awarded the Carnegie medal, the
*Guardian* Award and the Arts Council Award, and his
books have been translated into eight languages and have
been adapted as television serials.

# Leon Garfield

# Garfield's Apprentices
## book two

**The Cloak**
**The Valentine**
**Labour in Vain**

**illustrated by Faith Jaques**

**Piccolo** Pan Books
in association with Heinemann

*The Cloak* first published 1976, *The Valentine*
and *Labour in Vain* 1977, by William Heinemann Ltd
This edition published 1979 by Pan Books Ltd,
Cavaye Place, London SW10 9PG
in association with Heinemann
© Leon Garfield 1976, 1977
Illustrations © Faith Jaques 1976, 1977
ISBN 0 330 25647 5
Printed and bound in Great Britain by
Richard Clay (The Chaucer Press) Ltd, Bungay, Suffolk

# The Cloak

*to Vivien*

It was New Year's morning and nature, in a burst of good resolutions, had decided to begin with a clean slate – or about a million of them: snow had fallen heavily during the night. Everything was white; roofs, alleys, courts, lanes and streets looked as fresh and hopeful as a clean page awaiting the first entry . . .

A greasy old lamplighter, high on his ladder in Southampton Street, brooded on it all. He saw his own footprints and the marks made by his heavy ladder as he'd moved from lamp to lamp. Everything showed; even where he'd stumbled. He saw two kitchen maids hastening to fetch the morning's milk. He wished them a happy new year, and his voice, floating down through the silence imposed by the snow, startled them. They looked up with bright morning faces, wagged their fingers at the old man and laughingly returned his greeting.

The silence was uncanny; folk moved across the white

like toiling dreams. A gipsy woman with a laden donkey came down from Covent Garden way as soundlessly as a black thought.

Her face was dark, her hair was wild and she and her beast trudged up a little storm in the snow.

'Apples! Sweet Kent apples!' she cried as she saw the lamplighter. 'Who'll buy?'

She halted beside the ladder and turned her fierce eyes upward.

'No teeth,' said the lamplighter sadly. He gazed down and into the baskets the donkey patiently bore. In one lay a bushel of green and yellow apples; in the other, well wrapped in rags, slept a tiny baby, no more than a week old. The lamplighter grinned.

'But I must say, your little 'un looks soft enough to eat . . . even with poor, bare gums like these.'

He stretched back his lips in a kindly snarl.

'You can have her for a pound,' said the gipsy.

'Nowhere to put her, dear.'

'Fifteen shillings, then? Just so long as she goes to a good home.'

The lamplighter shook his head. He climbed down from his perch and, dipping his little finger into a tin of blacking he'd been gathering from the burnt remains of his lamps, reached into the basket and marked the top of the baby's head with a tiny cross.

'That's for luck, dear. Lamplighter's blacking; nought shall be lacking.'

'That's kind,' said the gipsy approvingly. 'Here's a sprig of white heather for you and yours. Gipsy's heather brings good weather. Where's the nearest pawnshop?'

'That's a bad way to start the new year, dear,' said the old man.

'Got to keep body and soul together,' countered the gipsy. 'Ain't I?'

The lamplighter scratched his head as he considered the problem.

"They won't take apples . . . nor babies, neither.'

'Got a garment,' said the woman proudly.

'They'll take that. Right off your back, if need be.'

'Will they?'

She stared into the lamplighter's cracked and ancient eyes. Suddenly he kindled up and grinned with an air of elderly mischief.

'Drury Lane, dear. Mr Thompson's.'

The gipsy returned the old man's smile.

'Rachel's blessing on you!' she called as she began to continue on her way.

'And a happy New Year!' answered the lamplighter, watching the woman and her donkey move soundlessly down the street, kicking up the snow in a fine spray so that it seemed they were walking upon a long white sea. It was just five minutes to eight o'clock.

At the southern end of Drury Lane, upon the left-hand side, stood the premises of Mr Thompson, Personal Banking at Moderate Terms. From a stout iron gibbet above the shop door hung the emblems of the trade: three brass balls that winked and gleamed in the wintry sunshine, beckoning to all in distress. Even on them the snow had settled, crowning them with caps of white so that they resembled three little round and shining brides of Christ.

Upon closer examination the brass balls did indeed

bear vague smudges like countenances, but not of a particularly radiant cast. Long ago, an actor (most of Mr Thompson's customers were on the stage, or temporarily off it) had climbed up and painted the masks of grim Tragedy on each of them; but time, weather, and the scrubbing brush of Coot, the apprentice, had worn them away to the merest ghosts of grief.

A rigid man, was Mr Thompson (and so was his brother-in-law, Mr Long, who pawnbroked in nearby Henrietta Street), and he conducted his business on the principle of the iron hand in the iron glove.

'A pawner is a man in difficulties,' he always warned his apprentice whenever he was called away and had to leave the shop in that youth's care. 'And a man in difficulties is a man in despair. Now despair, my boy, makes a man untrustworthy; it turns him into a liar, a swindler, a cheat. Poverty may not be a crime; but in my experience it's the cause of most of 'em. Poverty debases a man; and a base man is a man to keep a sharp eye on. It tells us in the Bible that it's hard enough for a rich man to enter the Kingdom of Heaven; so think how much harder it is for a poor one and the dishonest things he'll do to get there! He'll swear on his mother's grave that the article he's pawning is worth twice as much as ever we could sell it for. He'll give you his solemn word that it's only a loan and that he'll come back tomorrow and redeem it. We know those redeemers my boy. Like tomorrow, they never come. So you watch out!'

With these words Mr Thompson had left his apprentice as he and his brother-in-law, Mr Long, had gone off into the country for Christmas and the New Year. Then, recollecting that it was a festive season, had thought a joke to be in order.

'And if anyone comes,' he added, with a grisly twinkle in his eye, 'and wants to pawn a soul, you just send him down to Mr Long's! A merry Christmas, my boy; and if you watch out, a prosperous New Year!'

Accordingly the apprentice watched out; he watched out in ways, perhaps, that even his master never suspected.

He was a neat, thin youth of sixteen and was in the fourth year of his apprenticeship. He wore brass-rimmed spectacles (borrowed from stock), which lent him a studious air and enlarged his eyes which were, otherwise, inclined to be small and furtive.

Although the shop was not yet open, he was already

seated on his high stool in a discreet wooden cubby-hole that resembled a confessional, occupied in resting his elbows on the counter and making mysterious entries in a ledger. Beside him was a short piece of mahogany on which his name – Mister Coot – was painted in black; and beside that was a yellowed card announcing that: 'The House of Thompson wishes all its customers a Happy New Year.' It was kept in a small linen wallet and brought out every year.

Presently, having completed his entries, Coot gazed at the festive card and, with a jerk of inspiration, arranged the piece of mahogany over it to produce the heart-warming sentiment that, 'The House of Thompson wishes Mister Coot a Happy New Year.'

He sat for several minutes admiring it, then fished in his waistcoat pocket and came up with a massive silver watch secured to his person by means of a stout steel chain, like a criminal. He flicked up the lid and, observing that it lacked a minute till opening time, he thoughtfully picked his nose. At eight o'clock, Coot-time, he slipped from his stool, crawled under the counter and unbolted the door, returning with rat-like speed and dexterity lest a customer should catch him at a disadvantage. The House of Thompson was open to the new year.

The first customer was an ageing actor, hoping to raise five shillings on a pair of breeches not worth three.

'And – and a happy New Year to you!' he finished up, leaning over the counter with a mixture of affability and confidence through which despair showed in patches.

Coot smiled his pawnbroker's smile (which was next door to an undertaker's), and silently removed his name from the card, thereby returning the greeting and saving his breath.

He began to examine the breeches with fastidious care.

'Did I leave a guinea in it, old boy?' he asked with pathetic jocularity as Coot turned out the pocket.

Coot said nothing; he was watching out. He pushed the breeches back to their owner.

'Ay'm afraid they ain't much use to us. A bit too far gone.'

The actor was thunderstruck. He was outraged; he was humiliated; he was bitterly dismayed. He argued, he pleaded, he begged—

'All right. A shillin', then,' interposed Coot composedly, when he judged the customer to be sufficiently low in spirits to be agreeable to anything.

'A shilling? But—'

'Try Mr Long's in 'enrietta Street. P'raps my colleague, Mister Jeremiah Snipe, might up me a penny or two. On the other 'and, 'e might down me a sixpence. Go on. Shove off and try Mister Jeremiah.'

The pawnbroker's apprentice stared coolly at the customer, knowing him to be a beaten man. He wouldn't try Jeremiah – never in a month of Sundays! He wouldn't dare risk another such slap in the face. He was done for; he didn't even kick up much of a fuss when tuppence was knocked off his shilling: a penny for receipt and warehousing and a penny for two months' interest in advance.

'Really,' he muttered. 'That's a bit sharp, ain't it?'

For answer, Coot slid his eyes towards two framed notices that hung on the cubby-hole's wall. Decorated with the emblems of the trade, in the manner of illuminated missals, they set forth the rates of interest permitted by law, and the regulations designed to protect both parties, in a lending transaction, from the sharp practice of each other.

Wearily the actor shook his head. There was no sense in wasting his eyesight on the small print. Everything was above board, and the apprentice was as honest as an iron bar.

'I'll be back next week,' he said, taking his tenpence and mournfully patting his pawned garment, 'to redeem you, old friend.'

'Redeem?' You don't know the meanin' of the word,' murmured Coot, as the customer departed into the not quite new year.

Next came a fellow trying to pawn a wig, but the watchful apprentice found lice in it and sent him packing; and after him came a lady with the odd request that the apprentice should turn his back while she took off her petticoat hoops on which she wanted to borrow seven shillings.

'Turn me back?' said Coot, mindful of Mr Thompson's instruction to watch out. 'Ay'm afraid not. You might even nick me timepiece,' he said, laying that precious object (which his father had given him to mark the beginning of his apprenticeship) on the counter. 'I'll just sit as I am and not put temptation in your way.'

So the lady, with abject blushings, was forced to display her dirty linen and torn stockings to Coot's dreadful smile.

'Why – they ain't even real whalebone,' he said, when the hoops were offered across the counter. 'Ay'm afraid they ain't much use to us. Two shillin's. That's the best.'

'You dirty little skinflint!'

'Come to think on it,' said Coot, rightly taking the expression as a personal insult, 'a shillin' and ninepence is nearer the mark.'

He pushed the hoops back. 'Or you can try Mr Long's in 'enrietta Street. My colleague, Mister Jeremiah Snipe, might up me a penny or two. On the other 'and, 'e might down me a sixpence. Go on. Shove off and try Mister Jeremiah.'

He stared at her trembling lips and tear-filled eyes. She'd not try Jeremiah – never in a month of Sundays!

He was right, of course; he was always right; that was why Mr Thompson trusted him.

'I'll be back, of course,' said the lady, struggling to salvage some shreds of her self-respect, 'to redeem them next week.'

With that, she snatched up her shilling and ninepence

(less tuppence), and departed into the fast-ageing year.

Coot smiled and watched her through the window, noticing how her unsupported skirts dragged in the snow and wiped out her footprints even as she made them.

'Redeem?' he murmured. 'You don't know the meanin' of the word!'

He sat still for a moment, lost in philosophy; then he slipped from his stool, crawled under the counter and bolted the street door. Returning, he gathered up the hoops and breeches, ticketed them and carried them into the warehousing room at the back of the shop.

Here, in a dispiriting gloom that smelled of fallen fortunes, humbled pride and camphor to keep off the moth, they took their places amidst a melancholy multitude of pledges awaiting redemption. Wigs, coats, gowns and sheets, walking-sticks, wedding rings, shoes and watches waited in a long and doleful queue, as, month by month, they were moved up till, at the end of a year and a day, they were sold off, unredeemed.

It was a grim sight; but Coot, being in the trade, was not unduly moved by it. He surveyed the crowded racks and pigeon-holes and shelves.

'Redeemed?' he whispered. 'You don't know the meanin' of the word!'

When he arrived back, he found his cubby-hole as black as night; in his absence, a shadow, thick as a customer, seemed to have taken up residence.

'What the 'ell—' began the apprentice; then, craning his neck, he saw the gipsy woman at the window, obscuring the light.

She'd got her arms stretched out and was pressing her face and hands against the dirty glass as if to see what

was being offered for sale. She gave Coot quite a turn,
looming up like that; angrily, he waved her off.

She grinned at him and pointed to the sign that hung
over the door. Coot frowned; of all folk, gipsies needed
watching the most. Turn your back on them and they'd
have the buttons off your coat.

'Shove off!' he mouthed. 'And a 'orrible Noo Year!'

But the woman continued to grin, showing a set of
teeth much too good for her. She pointed to the sign
again and moved aside so that Coot could see her
donkey. Vigorously he shook his head.

'No livestock!' he shouted. 'Don't take 'em. Try Mr
Long's in 'enrietta Street!'

Now it was the gipsy's turn to shake her head, so Coot

unbolted the door and it opened by a crack. At once a sinewy brown hand came through and grasped the lintel. Coot glared at it and meditated slamming the door hard.

'Rachel's blessing on you, dear!' came the gipsy's harsh voice.

'Wotcher want?'

'Got something to pawn.'

'Nicked?'

'You know better than to ask that, dear!'

He did indeed. Nevertheless he had to watch out. Come to think of it, there wasn't much time left for watching out; Mr Thompson was due back in a couple of days.

'What is it, then?'

'Garment.'

Coot snorted. The gipsy stank like one o'clock. He'd not have advanced a sixpence on every stitch she stood up in – including whatever she wore underneath.

'Try Mr Long's in 'enrietta Street,' he said, and tried to shut the door.

'Real silk, dear,' said the gipsy. 'Fur collar and all. Worth a mint.'

Coot opened the door a further two inches and applied his eye to the gap, taking care to duck under the grasping hand. He saw that the woman was clutching a bundle under her free arm.

'That it?'

She laughed and tossed back a flap of the bundle. Coot saw the top of a baby's head. There was a black mark on it.

'Don't you bring that in 'ere,' said Coot nervously. 'It's got somethin' nasty.'

'But it's cold out here.'

'You should have thought on that before. You gipsies ain't fit to 'ave babies. It don't come in 'ere.'

To Coot's surprise, the gipsy nodded meekly and returned the baby to its basket. Then she came back carrying a black article that she'd removed from one of the bundles on the donkey. It was silk, sure enough.

'All right,' he said, letting go of the door and bolting back to his place with his customary neatness and speed. But as he settled on his stool, he couldn't help feeling that she'd been too quick for him and come in while he was still at a disadvantage.

Silently the garment was passed over the counter and Coot began to examine it. It was a cloak of black silk with a violet lining. The collar was real fox fur, and round the inside of the neck there was some delicate embroidery. It certainly was a handsome article; but nevertheless, the pawnbroker's apprentice knew he had to watch out.

''ow did you come by it?'

'It was my father's, dear.'

'Oh yes. Your father's.' Coot grinned knowingly.

'My father's!' repeated the woman, with a touch of anger.

'Where are you from?' pursued Coot. 'Got to ask on account of the law.'

'Kent.'

'That's a long way off.'

'T'other side o' the moon!'

'Far enough, eh?' said Coot, meaningly.

The woman nodded. 'Far enough, dear.'

''ow much was you expectin' on this garment?'

'Two silver pounds, dear.'

'And the rest! D'you think I'm off me 'ead? Two pound to a thievin' old thing like you? You're 'avin' me on! Two pound for a bit of furry rubbish like this? Take a look at it . . . take a good look! Moth in the collar like nobody's business! And what about this stitchin'? Won't last out a week! And – look 'ere! Dirty great stain that won't come out in a month of Sundays!' (There was indeed a rusty brown stain on the violet lining, though it was not a large one.) 'And the 'ole garment whiffs something awful. Never get that smell off it! If I was to let you 'ave five shillin's on this, I'd be doin' you a favour and meself an injury.'

'Only five shillings, dear? I was hoping, I was counting on more than that. I got my little one to care for.'

'Like I said, my good woman, you should 'ave thought on that before. Five shillin's is the 'ouse's best.'

'A pound, dear. Make it a silver pound!'

'Why don't you shove off? Try Mr Long's in 'enrietta Street. Maybe my colleague, Mister Jeremiah, might up me a penny or two. On the other 'and, 'e might down me a sixpence. Go on. Shove off!'

'Ten shillings! Give me ten silver shillings!'

'Five. What would my master say if I was to give you over the odds? 'e'd'ave me out quicker'n a dose of rhubarb! You want to do me down, you do! Five shillin's – or I send for the constable!'

This was Coot's masterstroke. The woman's eyes widened and she began to tremble. He'd got her!

'All right, then – all right!' she muttered. 'Give me the five shillings and a receipt.'

'Receipt? What do you want that for?'

'To – to redeem my cloak. I – I'm coming back for it . . . soon.'

'Redeem?' said Coot. 'You don't know the meanin' of the word!'

But the gipsy insisted with all the obstinate ignorance of her tribe; so Coot chuckled and wrote out a receipt.

'That'll cost you another threepence,' he said, giving her the money and packing her off out of the shop.

When she was safely out of sight, he bolted the door and examined the cloak again. He tried it on, but it was far too big for him, and covered him like a shroud. He tried lifting a corner and flinging it over his shoulder, in the manner of an ancient Roman; but it really wasn't his style. Regretfully he took it off, noticing that the rusty stain was on the left-hand side and would, had he been of a height, have covered his heart; as it was, it rested over his sweetbread. Thoughtfully he stroked the fur collar and looked again at the embroidery round the inside of the neck. He pursed his lips; then he grinned broadly. The embroidery was not, as he'd first supposed, a pattern; it was instead a line of Gothic letters making up a text.

'I KNOW THAT MY REDEEMER LIVETH,' said the pawned cloak.

'That's what they all say!' chuckled the pawn-broker's apprentice. 'But they don't know the meanin' of the word!'

By half past seven in the evening, the brave New Year was torn to tatters. No more snow had fallen and clean white streets were crossed and double-crossed by the black passing of men and women going about their daily affairs.

Freed from toil, the pawnbroker's apprentice chose to walk where the snow had been well trodden down. He was wearing his best shoes and did not want to spoil them; also, perhaps, at the back of his watchful mind was the thought that it was best to leave no footprints as his journey would not bear the closest examination.

He walked with a springy step, quite like a young lamb; it was as if all his hours of grimly patient dealing had compressed him like a spring, so that now he leaped forth with a youthful twang. He was done up to the nines, wearing a dazzling waistcoat, a ginger wig and silken breeches of egg-yolk yellow. He was a butterfly; he was a youth transformed.

Presently he reached Henrietta Street and gave a smart double knock on the door of Mr Long's (Loans Arranged on Modest Security): and while he waited,

winked up knowingly at the three brass balls. J. Snipe
opened the door.

'A 'appy Noo Year, Jerry!'

'Same to you, Cooty. And with three brass knobs on!'

Jeremiah, who was renowned for his wit, smirked as
he stepped aside to admit his colleague and friend. He
was a month younger than Coot and of a round-faced,
angelic appearance that tended to make his customers
feel ashamed of bargaining with him. But there lurked
under that soft exterior a spirit every bit as stern as
Coot's. Well, perhaps not quite so stern as he'd been in
the trade four weeks less than his friend; but he was
catching up fast.

'You've got something, haven't you, Cooty?'

Coot beamed.

'Thought so,' said Jeremiah shrewdly. 'That's why
you're done up like the cat's dinner.'

'Take a squint at this,' said Coot, ignoring his colleague's wit. 'Gipsy brought it.'

He produced the cloak. Jeremiah whistled, then crawled under his counter so that he might examine the article from his usual situation. Coot made to follow him when he saw Jeremiah's boot defensively poised; so he stayed the wrong side of the counter reflecting that, whenever positions were reversed, he defended his own territory in the same way.

'Five pound,' said Jeremiah, when he had finished studying the garment.

'Don't you come the skinflint with me, Jerry,' said Coot affably. 'Make it six.'

Jeremiah smiled like an angel in a stained-glass window – a very stained-glass window – and nodded. 'Six it is, then.'

Agreement having been thus reached, the two industrious apprentices settled down to complete the necessary business of their interesting arrangement. As was required by law, Jeremiah noted down the transaction in Mr Long's ledger, while Coot did the same in his own ledger which had nothing to do with the law. Then Jeremiah handed over six pounds of Mr Long's money, less the cost of warehousing, receipting and two months' interest in advance; as was permitted by law. This done, Coot handed back to Jeremiah half of the proceeds, as was demanded by the terms of their partnership and the liability of their friendship.

'It's not as if we was thieves,' Coot had said to Jeremiah when the idea had first come to him and Jeremiah had cast doubts on its honesty. 'We're just business men. We ain't reely breakin' the law. You might say we ain't even goin' close enough to touch

it! Look at it this way, Jerry,' he'd gone on, feeling that his colleague remained unconvinced. 'Think of bankers.'

'Well?'

'They're lawful, ain't they?'

'According to their lights.'

'Well, then – you put your money in a bank—'

'—I don't. I keep it in my shoe.'

'I was just supposin'. You put your money in a bank, and then the bank goes and does all sorts of things with it. Lends it out, invests it, buy things with it . . . and generally treats it like the money was its own. And that's what we'll be doin'. Folk pawn articles with us, and we pawn 'em again to each other. We're only borrerin' and lendin' out at interest. We ain't stealin', we're just re-investin'. And as long as nobody catches on, we'll end up in pocket. Bound to.'

'But what if they *do* catch on?' asked Jeremiah, filled with something of the foreboding of the ancient prophet whose name he bore.

'It won't 'appen,' had said Coot firmly. 'Never in a month of Sundays. It'd need more rotten luck than we got a right to expect. Listen, Jerry: in business, you got to take some chances. I'm more experienced than you. Just let me do the worryin' and be 'appy to take the money. That's all I ask.'

So Jeremiah, borne down by Coot's arguments, and borne up by the prospect of income, agreed. All this had taken place a year ago, since when the two industrious apprentices had prospered exceedingly, being careful to transact their private business when their masters were out of town. It was for such opportunities that Coot and

Jeremiah obeyed their masters more fully than they suspected, by watching out.

'Where shall we go tonight, Cooty?' asked Jeremiah, when he had ticketed and stowed away the cloak in his master's warehouse room.

'Ay raither fancy the Hopera,' said Coot, with extreme cultivation. 'So get your rags on . . . and don't forget your claret pot.'

The pot referred to was Jeremiah's silver christening mug that occupied, in his affections, a similar place to the great silver timepiece in Coot's.

At a quarter past eight o'clock the two apprentices left Henrietta Street for their night on the town. They marched in step, as if an invisible band was playing – just for them. They were smart, they were elegant, they were dapper. They gladdened the heart and imparted a youthful gaiety to the precincts of Bow Street. Their eyes sparkled, their shoe-buckles twinkled, so there was brightness at both ends, and money in the middle.

To begin with, they took in – as Coot put it – the second act of the opera. They went up into the gallery where, with footmen, students and other lively apprentices, they whistled and hooted and clapped, cheered on the lady performers and threw oranges down on bare heads in the pit till they were requested to leave or take the consequences. Then they went to a respectable inn and got mildly drunk on claret and port; after which Jeremiah was sick on the pavement and Coot fell into the snow. Partly recovered, they found a cock-fight in Feathers Court and lost ten shillings each on a bird that lay down before it was so much as tickled. Then they joined up with half a dozen weavers' apprentices and had a tremendous time trying to steal door-knockers and pelting a pursuing constable with stones disguised as snowballs.

They parted with the weavers' apprentices – who'd run out of money – and took up with a couple of likely lasses who'd caught their roving eyes in the Strand. They told the girls they were soldiers on leave and that they'd been wounded in the foreign wars. They limped a bit to prove it . . . then kissed and cuddled and bought the girls supper in Maiden Lane, lording it over the waiter till the wretched man felt like pouring hot soup over the apprentices' heads.

But he did no such thing and Coot tipped him well to impress the girls with his careless generosity.

Coot and Jeremiah were firm believers in keeping business and pleasure apart. Though Coot would have fought with a cringing customer to the last breath in his body to beat him down by a shilling, he thought nothing at all of casting such a shilling (and two others like it) into the waiter's greasy palm. And Jeremiah who, with crocodile tears, would have denied a customer an extra penny, happily filled and refilled his silver tankard with wine, spilling it on the table and in his lap, at three-pence a throw.

At last the two bright apprentices tottered back towards Drury Lane, quite worn out from their night on the town. They'd broken windows, tipped an old watchman into a horse-trough and unscrewed a lamp from a standing coach. They'd lost their lasses some-where round the back of Covent Garden, and they'd not a penny left to bless themselves with; but they were happy and singing, and they kicked on front doors as

they passed, with night-piercing screeches of "'appy Noo Year!'

'Look!' hiccuped Jeremiah, staring boozily down Drury Lane. 'You got a customer, Cooty!'

Coot blinked and stared. Several figures seemed to be outside Mr Thompson's, and they were on fire; flames were coming up all round them. Coot wiped his eyes and the figures reduced themselves to two: a tall man and a link-boy who had, presumably, guided him there. The link-boy's torch leaped and danced and illuminated the three brass balls in a manner that was quite uncanny; the masks of Tragedy fairly glowered down.

Dazedly, Coot gazed upon the scene, then shouted out:

'Shove off! We ain't open till eight o'clock!'

The customer saluted him, but did not move; so Coot pursued a winding, uncertain path to confront him and make his meaning clearer. The link-boy, seeing the angry apprentice, bolted and left the street to the feeble memory of his light.

'I told you,' said Coot, squaring up to the customer in the manner of a weaving prizefighter, 'we're shut. Closed. No business, see? All gone bye-bye. Shove off and come back in the mornin'.'

The stranger, who was a good twelve inches taller than the pawnbroker's apprentice, looked down sombrely. There was something nasty about the man; he had a hooked nose like a vulture and eyes that seemed to keep shifting about all over his face. Coot took a step back, and bumped into Jeremiah, who had been sheltering behind him.

Suddenly the stranger reached into his pocket; and Coot, who was expecting a knife or a pistol, endeavoured

to get behind his colleague. But the stranger only produced a slip of paper.

'Wassat?'

'Don't you recognize it?' inquired the stranger, harshly.

"ow can I recko'nize it when you keeps wavin' it about?'

'It's a receipt.'

'Reely? You don't say.'

'It's a receipt for a cloak. You gave it to a gipsy woman this morning. She pawned the cloak with you for five shillings.'

'Well, what of it?' said Coot valiantly. Events were moving a little too quickly for him quite to grasp their significance.

'It wasn't hers.'

'Nicked? What an 'orrible thing. I'm sorry to 'ear it. Them gipsies! Night-night!'

'It was mine. I gave it out for cleaning. I can prove it was mine. There was a text inside the collar. 'I know that my Redeemer liveth.' I am that redeemer, my friend. I want my cloak back. Either that, or I fetch a magistrate to search your premises and examine your books. That's the law, my friend. So bring out the cloak.'

Coot felt Jeremiah beside him begin to shake and tremble like a straw in a tempest. Although he couldn't see him, he knew his face had gone dead white and that he was crying; he always did.

But he, Coot, was made of sterner stuff; four weeks sterner. Delay, that was it. Put off the evil hour and it might never come to pass. There was no sense in meeting trouble half way. Far better to step aside and let it go rampaging past.

He informed the stranger that, at that precise moment, the cloak in question was in the firm's warehouse which, unfortunately, was some distance away. It couldn't be helped, and he, Coot, sympathised with the gent's annoyance. But that was how things were, and nothing was to be gained by crying over spilt milk. He would do his very best to obtain the garment in the course of a day or two. He couldn't speak fairer than that.

Just what was in Coot's complicated mind was hard to say. Perhaps he thought the stranger was a bad dream from which he would awaken if only given the time?

'I want my cloak now,' said the stranger, refusing to behave like a dream. 'Either that, or pay me the value of the garment. Ten pounds. The cloak, ten pounds – or the law.'

At this point, Jeremiah spoke up. His voice fell upon the night like the wail of his namesake, the prophet, deploring the loss of Jerusalem.

'Give him the ten pound, Cooty! For God's sake, give him the ten pounds!'

The worst had happened, like he'd always known it would. The rotten luck that was more than they'd any right to expect, had befallen them. They were done for.

'And where am I goin' to get the ten pound?' snarled Coot, turning on his friend who retreated several paces, weeping bitterly.

'I don't know – I don't know!'

'Pardon me,' said Coot to the stranger, who appeared to be relishing the friends' predicament. 'Ay wish to consult with may colleague on business.'

He joined Jeremiah.

'Keep your voice down!'

'Give him the ten pounds, then!'

'Can't. You give 'im the cloak.'

'But I lent six pounds on it! How am I going to account for that? Old Long comes back the day after tomorrow!'

'So does old Thompson! And six pound is easier to find than ten.'

'But I'll have to find it! You'll just be dropping me in it, won't you Cooty?'

Coot laid a hand on Jeremiah's shoulder, as much to steady himself as to reassure his colleague.

'We're in it together, Jerry. We'll find a way. You just see if we don't. It'd take more rotten luck than we got a right to expect if we didn't manage some'ow. For Gawd's sake, Jerry, give 'im back the cloak!'

'You'll help, then?'

'I swear it. On me mother's grave,' muttered Coot, forgetful of the fact that his mother was not yet in it. He returned to the stranger.

'We are sorry to 'ave hinconvenienced you,' he said coldly, 'but the garment was taken in good faith. We – I 'ad no idea the garment was nicked. 'owever, hunder the circs. we are prepared to return your property at no hextra charge. My colleague and I will—'

'At once!' interrupted the stranger, 'or I go for the magistrate!'

'If you was a smaller man,' said Coot venomously, 'I'd punch you right in the nose!'

'Six pounds!' wept Jeremiah. 'How are we going to find it?' The cloak had been given up and the friends were still in Mr Long's shop.

'Don't you worry, Jerry,' said Coot. 'I'll come up with somethin'. I've never let you down yet.'

'You've never had the chance!'

'Now that weren't friendly, Jerry. But I'll look after you.'

'You'd better, Cooty. You'd better!'

'What do you mean by that?'

'If I go to jail, so do you. There's other things, you know. If I get caught on this one, you get caught on the others. Don't you think I'm going down alone. You always said we were in it together.'

'That's nasty, Jerry. Particularly as you've always been 'appy to sit back and enjoy the money I thought of gettin'. But I don't 'old it against you. You're younger than me. All I want you to consider is that . . . well . . . what's the sense in both of us goin' down when it need only be one? Wouldn't it be better if one of us stayed safe so's 'e could 'elp the other when the time came?'

'All right. You take the blame and I'll help you when you come out of jail.'

'Point taken,' said Coot. 'But the money 'appens to be missin' from your 'ouse, not mine. Otherwise I'd be 'appy to oblige.'

Jeremiah began to cry again; then, seeing that his tears had no effect, grew exceedingly angry. He made it plain that he did not trust Coot. Coot had got him into it, and Coot was going to get him out. Or suffer by his side.

At last, Coot was forced to see how matters stood. Jeremiah was taking advantage of previous acts of friendship and was holding them against him. He just wasn't capable of distinguishing between business and pleasure.

'If that's the way it's to be,' he said bitterly, 'we got to lay our 'ands on six pounds; and another five shillin's, which is the hamount I'm in to Mr Thompson.'

'And before the day after tomorrow,' said Jeremiah, anticipating any attempt to delay.

'Six pounds ain't a fortune,' went on Coot, ignoring the interruption. 'As I see it, there's reely only two ways of gettin' it. We could either borrer it – or nick it.'

'I ain't stealing,' said Jeremiah quickly. He felt that it was in Coot's mind for him, Jeremiah, to do the nicking. 'You can get hung for that.'

'Point taken,' said Coot. 'No nickin' on account of the risk. Although—'

'Any stealing you can do yourself, Cooty.'

'Like I said, no nickin'. That leaves borrerin'.'

'Who'd lend us six pounds, Cooty?'

'Good question. What about pawnin' more of the stock to each other?'

'I've had enough of that. We're sure to get found out.'

Coot sighed and stared at his over-cautious associate. His eye fell upon Jeremiah's christening mug.

'All right,' he said slowly. 'Seein' as 'ow you've taken things out of my 'ands, you can do somethin' yourself for a change. 'ow about pawnin' that pot of yours?'

Jeremiah began to cry again. Tears ran out of his eyes as fast as melting snow. Contemptuously, Coot waited.

'You're a pig, Cooty,' sobbed Jeremiah at length. 'Take it, then; and give me the six pounds!'

'Six pounds?' said Coot. 'Ay'm afraid,' he began, from force of habit; and then corrected himself. 'Climb down a bit, Jerry. You know I daren't make it six. Old Thompson goes through the books like a dog through a dust 'eap when 'e gets 'ome. 'e'd never stand for six pound! Not for an old piece of Sheffield plate with scratches all over it!'

'It's not plate! It's solid silver! I wasn't christened in plate!'

'Tell us another, Jerry! Look at it! Copper showin' through everywhere, plain as a baby's bum. Two pound is the very best. Solid silver my eye!'

'You're a dirty rotten liar, Cooty! Make it four pound, then?'

'I daren't, Jerry. It's more than me place is worth. Tell you what, though. I'll make it two pound ten shillin's and that'll only leave you three pound ten to find. There, now; don't say I ain't comin' up trumps. That's what I call real friendship!'

'And that's what I call dirty swindling, Cooty. You're not leaving here till all the money's made up. If you do, you be right in it alongside of me. You can pawn your watch . . .'

'Me timepiece?' cried Coot, shocked to the core. 'But it's a valuable hobject. No . . . I couldn't do that.'

'Then it's jail for the both of us.'

'Do you know you're bein' very nasty, Jerry? And 'ard. I never thought you was so 'ard underneath.'

'Your watch, Cooty. Come on. Let's have a look.'

Silently Coot withdrew the gleaming article.

'This 'ere timepiece is worth – is worth fifteen pound if it's worth a penny,' he said sorrowfully. 'You're takin' an 'ammer to crack a egg, Jerry.'

'Pass it over, Cooty.'

Coot released his treasure from its chain and laid it on Jeremiah's counter. Jeremiah fell to examining it closely.

'Fifteen pound? Oh dear me, no! Old Long would

have me committed for life if I was to go along with that,' said Jeremiah. Like Coot, he had good reason to fear his master's scrutiny of the books; and also he was still smarting under Coot's treatment of his christening mug.

'If I was to give you two pounds, I'd be stretchin' it, Cooty.'

'Two pound? You dirty little skinflint!' shouted Coot, banging on the counter so that the watch jumped in alarm. Jeremiah folded his arms.

'To begin with,' he said, 'it ain't silver. It's only pewter. And what's more, it's stopped ever since you dropped it earlier on. And it's all scratched and dented like a tinker's spoon. That there chain's worth more than the watch.'

'That there timepiece was give me by my pa!' said Coot, savagely. 'I wouldn't be pawnin' it but to 'elp *you*! Come on! Give us twelve pound!'

'You'll take two pound ten shillings,' said Jeremiah coldly. 'Just like me.'

'You lousy rotten stinking little skinflint!' raged Coot, attempting to regain possession of his watch. 'I'd sooner rot in jail than be treated like this! Oh for Gawd's sake, Jerry, make it nine pound and call it a day? Please, Jerry! It's me pa's watch! It's valuable to me . . . It – it's all I got in the world!'

'Two pound ten,' said Jeremiah. 'Less warehousing, of course.'

'You're cuttin' off your own nose, Jerry. You're cuttin' your own throat.'

'And yours, Cooty,' said Jeremiah, not without satisfaction.

'What about the other pound and five shillin's?'

'I'll take your weskit for half of it; and you can take my new coat for the rest. That's fair.'

'Your coat, Jerry, it pains me to tell you, ain't worth more'n two shillin's. I'll 'ave your best shoes, too!'

'I don't like you, Cooty.'

'Nor me you, Jerry. And I never 'ave.'

Following on this frightful revelation, there was a longish pause.

'But it's been worth it,' said Jeremiah, finally. He had been brooding on how he might display, even more crushingly, his contempt for Coot. 'Yes. I don't begrudge the experience. It's shown you up, Cooty. I'm glad to have paid to see you, really to see you. I've had a narrow escape, Cooty. I might have turned out like you, if I hadn't seen what you're like underneath.'

'Likewise,' said Coot, determined to outdo Jeremiah. 'And what's more, I'd willin'ly 'ave paid out double to see what I 'ave just seen. 'orrible. Made me sick to me stomach. You're the sort, Jerry, what gets 'uman bein's a bad name. Thank Gawd I found out in time.'

Jeremiah, who could come up with nothing better for the moment, opened the shop door and indicated that his colleague's presence was no longer welcome. Breathing heavily, the two apprentices stood in the doorway. Coot thought of punching Jeremiah in the face. He shook his head. He recollected, 'Vengeance is mine; I will repay, saith the Lord.' He stared up and saw the weighty emblem of Mr Long's trade poised above Jeremiah's head. 'Go on, God!' he thought. 'Fix 'im!' But the three brass balls remained stolidly in the air.

'And don't you go sending me any of your customers any more,' said Jeremiah, having thought of something else. 'Because I'll tell them what a grinding little skinflint you are. I'll show you up. If you send them to me, I'll give them what they ask for.'

'And I'll give 'em more!' said Coot furiously. 'Just for the pleasure of hexposin' you! I wouldn't send a dog to you, Jerry!'

'If I could find that gipsy,' quavered Jeremiah, stung to the quick; 'I'd get down on my hands and knees and thank her for letting me see the truth.'

'I might remind you,' said Coot loftily, 'that I'm the one she came to. I'm the one what was chosen to be redeemed.'

Jeremiah breathed deeply.

'Garn!' he said. 'You don't know the meaning of the word!'

Slowly Coot made his way back to Drury Lane. A church clock began to strike midnight; the New Year was past. Unthinkingly Coot fumbled for his watch to see if the church was right. No watch; no waistcoat, even. He shivered as he felt the cold strike through.

Snow had begun to fall again: tiny flakes that pricked and glittered as they passed through the feeble rays of the street lamps. Little by little, as the snow settled, the black scars and furrows that marked the road lost their sharpness and seemed to fade. Presently they were reduced to smudgy ghosts, like rubbed out entries in a ledger.

By the time he reached Drury Lane, the snow was fairly whirling down and he was as white as the street. The flakes kept stinging him in the eyes so that he could scarcely see where he was going.

It was under these circumstances that he saw the apparition; and considering how much he'd drunk and what he'd been through, it wasn't surprising. He saw the Holy Family.

Out of the snow they came: the laden donkey, the radiant mother and the tall, saintly man beside her. Coot crossed himself as they drew near.

'Buy an apple, dear!' called out the gipsy woman. 'Buy a sweet Kent apple for good luck!'

'A happy New Year! A happy New Year, my boy!' called out the man by her side.

He was the stranger, the hook-nosed stranger, stalking along in his treacherous, ruinous black silk cloak!

They'd been in it together – the pair of them! They'd done him! They'd swindled him! They'd stripped him bare! The thieves! The rogues! The rotten, crafty swindlers! They were all in it . . . most likely the baby and the donkey, too!

Coot stood as still as a post; and then began to shake and tremble with indignation. Helplessly he watched them pass him by and then vanish like a dream into the whirling curtain of snow.

Then he gathered together his tattered shreds of self-respect and reflected on many things.

'I suppose it were worth it,' he whispered. 'All things considered, I suppose it were worth it in the end.'

With aching head and shaking hands, he unlocked the door of Mr Thompson's (Personal Banking at Moderate Terms), and let himself in.

He leaned across the counter, staring into the dark emptiness, which was his place in life.

'If anybody comes in to pawn a soul,' he whispered,

remembering his master's little joke, 'just you send 'em down to Mr Long's! But what if,' he went on, smiling mournfully to himself, 'they comes in to redeem one?'

He went to the door again and opened it. He stared out into the teeming weather. Although the little family had long since gone, he fancied he saw them imprinted on the ceaseless white. He tried to recollect their features – the man, the woman, the tiny child. But they were just shapes, haunting shapes that left no footprints; all that remained was a vague perfume of apples and spice.

'Try my colleague in 'enrietta Street,' he called softly into the night. 'Go on; try Mister Jeremiah, my friend.'

# The Valentine

*to Daisy and John*

Not very far from Jessop & Pottersfield's in Little Knightrider Street, is St Martin's Churchyard where wicked children hide among the headstones, waiting to nick any wreaths and sell them back to the undertakers. Horrible, unfeeling trade! but even in the midst of death life must go on!

One cold bright morning in February (it was the fourteenth, but they didn't know it), three such shrunken malevolents played and darted among the dead, like apprentice spooks . . .

'Look out – look out! There's summ'un comin'!'

Instantly they vanished behind the tombs and crouched trembling in the freezing grass as the Lady in Black drifted towards them over the green. They quaked. What was she? Was she a witch, a spirit, a ghost . . . ?

They'd seen her before: she haunted the churchyard, and one grave in particular . . . the one under the shadow of the bent elder tree. They'd heard that every

St Valentine's Day she brought a wreath of flowering ivy and wild garlic.

Sure enough, they saw she carried a wreath and their interest quickened. She was deeply, impenetrably veiled, and only the dim sparkle of her eyes could be seen as she approached and paused by the graveside, glancing first at the overhanging bough, and then down to the smooth coverlet of grass. Quickly she knelt and laid the wreath against the headstone.

'Get a move on!' breathed the tiny watchers, perishing from stillness and cold. 'Get a move on, can't yer?'

But the Lady in Black remained in her prayerful attitude for several minutes, as if longing to be translated into stone and stay for ever by the grave under the elder tree. Only a faint trembling of her veil betrayed that she was still alive; she was whispering to whoever lay under the grass.

At length she rose and drifted out of the churchyard with a step as silent and light as thistledown. The wreath remained behind . . .

'Quick!'

'What if 'e's watchin' ?'

' 'oo ?'

' 'im, down under!'

'Garn!'

'Look! The grass moved!'

'It were the wind.'

'But what if it were 'im, turnin' over?'

'All right, I'll ask 'im. Did yer turn over, mister?'

The three demons held their breath, and one of them pressed his ear to the ground. There was no answer.

'Don't you mind us, mister. It's nuffink personal. It's just that we got to live anyways we can.'

Six feet below, Orlando Brown, who had been taken from this life in his sixteenth year, deeply loved and much missed, held his tongue as his lonely tribute and remembrance went the way of young flesh and was heartlessly nicked . . .

Jessop & Pottersfield had buried him on St Valentine's Day, just five years ago. They'd done it handsomely and tastefully . . . which was a sight more than Alfred Todds's would have done had the business gone their way; but luckily that was before Messrs Todds had employed the odious Hawkins.

Hawkins was a nothing, a nobody, a lean, scraggy undertaker's lad so anxious to get on in life (which was comical considering his trade!) that he made himself ridiculous in the district – ridiculous and dreaded!

The very sight of him in his outgrown blacks (he seemed to keep on sprouting like a stick of starved celery), hanging about at street corners, eavesdropping on gossip and following physicians and midwives, made cold shivers run up and down your spine. He made folk uneasy, especially the old and the sick. He was like a gleaner in the cobbled fields, waiting for the grim Reaper so he might gather in the fallen sheaves.

His eager knock and his low, horribly respectful voice: 'Mr Todds tenders his sincerest condolences, and might he have the honour of furnishing the funeral?' made you sick that anyone could stoop so low in the way of business.

These were the feelings of Miss Jessop, lovely daughter of Jessop & Pottersfield's. She loathed and

despised Hawkins, who, despite his undeniably dreamy eyes and long, poetical hands (with fingernails permanently wearing the livery of the trade), was coarse and pushing and always picking up custom where he had no right to.

The Lord alone knew where Todds's had found him; on some rubbish heap, most likely; but he'd taken to the trade with a passion and zeal that were quite unnatural. He'd worked his fingers to the bone (and they looked it!) for Todds's, scrubbing their dreary yard, washing the customers, running errands for their drunken joiner (who couldn't put a screw in straight to save his life!), polishing the lamps on the hearse and then managing to turn out in time for the funeral, glossy as a beetle in his working blacks. At first he carried a branch of candles; but then when he kept sprouting, he took a turn at bearing. You could always pick out his spiky shanks, coming and going under the pall.

'That lad's a gem,' boasted Mr Todds to Mr Jessop. 'Mark my words, he'll go far!'

And he did go far. In fact he went right to the confines of Little Knightrider Street and poached trade right out of Jessop & Pottersfield's very pockets. Sometimes Miss Jessop felt that were her ma and pa to drop dead tomorrow, Hawkins would be at the door within the hour, murmuring:

'Mr Todds tenders his sincerest condolences, miss, and might he have the honour of furnishing the funeral?'

So strongly did Miss Jessop feel this, that there were times when she almost exploded with fury. The worst of it was that people, good, ordinary people, really were taken in by the loathsome Hawkins and his 'sincerest condolences'. They stopped their dazed weeping for long enough to nod and leave everything to Messrs Todds, without a thought for the fact that they might have done better elsewhere. It's a melancholy truth that, in times of bereavement when the undertaker ought to come into his own as he is the only one standing upright while others are lying distraught upon couches, nobody thinks of asking a friend or a neighbour, 'Is he the best to be had?'

Recommendation goes for nothing. Alas, it's not a trade like butchery or haberdashery that enjoys a regular family custom. Generally speaking, folk only get buried once, and are in no situation to praise or complain about the service.

Consequently – and thanks to Hawkins's pushing ways – Todds's now furnished nine out of every ten funerals in the district, while Jessop & Pottersfield's, discreet, courteous Jessop & Pottersfield's, languished in circumstances that, daily, grew as straitened as the sides of a coffin.

Little by little economies were forced upon the once well-to-do household: servants were let go and Miss Jessop herself had to give up music, painting, needle-work and French. Then even the outside boy was dis-charged. Miss Jessop was deeply sorry to see him go. He promised to write to her, but he never did; instead he bequeathed her the odious tasks that had once been his. To her now fell the disagreeable lot of intruding on other folks' grief in order to get their business.

Dressed in her father's solemn livery, she'd wait, day after day, outside houses where there was known to be sickness. Anxiously she'd watch the windows, waiting for the blinds to be drawn. But more often than not, she was too much of a lady to be in at the death, as they say, with the vulgar promptitude of a Hawkins. With an aching heart she heard:

'I'm sorry, miss, but we're already suited. Mr Todds is looking after us.'

'Pray – pray accept our sincere condolences,' she'd murmur with a rueful nod, indicating, perhaps, more sorrow for the family's choice than for their loss. Then she'd hasten away to the sympathetic accompaniment of:

'Lovely lass, that. What a pity she's in the under-taking line!'

Yes; she was only an undertaker's daughter, but she wore her blacks with a difference. They became her like the night. Yet she was neither betrothed nor even courted. Hers was a trade in which she was fated to blush and bloom unseen. An undertaker's circle of friends is sorely limited: a joiner or two, an unlucky physician, a sexton and maybe a dusty old monumental mason; so the beautiful Miss Jessop walked alone and ate out her heart with tears and a strange, fantastic dream.

'O death, where is thy sting?' she wept into her pillow each night. 'O grave, where is thy victory?'

Then she'd dry her eyes as her aching bosom made answer:

'In St Martin's Churchyard. Under the elder tree.'

She was in love with Orlando Brown, who had entered her father's shop one February 13th, and had gone out of it on St Valentine's Day, never to return.

It had happened in the days of prosperity, long before the appearance of Hawkins, when Miss Jessop had been a tempestuous eleven, much given to moods, passionate affections and violent disagreements with the household.

It had been following one such disagreement, when she had been confined to her room without supper until she saw fit to beg her mother's pardon, that she had grown so excessively hungry that she risked her father's anger and crept forth to visit the solemn front parlour which, ordinarily, she shunned like the plague.

This parlour, with its mahogany side-table, its massive candelabra and its black velvet curtains, served as a Chapel of Rest for those who, for one reason and another, were not to be buried from their own homes. Often, busy tradesmen did not care to keep a departed one on the premises with customers continually coming and going; so at night a long black cart (which Miss Jessop always remembered as having a disagreeable smell) called at the bereaved's and returned to Jessop & Pottersfield's.

She knew there were often biscuits and wine in the parlour to sustain any mourners who called to make their last adieus. It was the thought of this that gave her the necessary courage.

She stiffened her sinews, clenched her fists and pushed open the door. Within, all was bright with candlelight. She saw, with pleasure and relief, that there were honey cakes in little black paper cups laid out on a pewter dish on the side-table; but at the same time she saw that there was a coffin upon trestles in the middle of the room.

The draught from the open door disturbed the candle flames so that everything in the room seemed to be moving. Resolutely she averted her eyes from the coffin and fixed them on the side-table. But it was no use; she couldn't help seeing, out of the corner of her eye, that the coffin was open and that there was *someone* inside it.

Seized with a wholly unreasonable fear, due, most likely, to her feelings of guilt, she paused. Then, carefully marking the direction of the side-table and honey cakes, she shut her eyes as tightly as she could and began to fumble her way across the room.

Presently she felt the side-table press up against her. She sighed with relief. She reached forward, stretching out her fingers to feel the cold edge of the pewter plate. Where had it gone? Slowly she lowered her hand. Ah! Something cold . . . something very cold.

She opened her eyes; and try as she might, she could not shut them again.

She was not leaning against the side-table, nor was she touching the pewter plate. She was pressed against

the coffin, and her hand was resting upon the waxy white fingers of Orlando Brown!

The dancing candlelight played uncanny tricks with his quiet eyelids and his grey lips. He was smiling at her . . .

Miss Jessop screamed and snatched back her hand. She forgot the honey cakes, she forgot everything and rushed from the parlour, consumed with sickness and dread.

She reached her room and plunged into her bed where she lay, entirely under the covers, as still as Orlando Brown himself. But it was no use; neither sheets nor blankets, had they been a mile thick, could have shut out the image of the dead youth's face. Orlando Brown kept smiling at her from every corner in her head; he kept smiling gently, gravely . . .

'No – no – no! Go away from me!'

Her fingers could still feel the icy touch of his; she

rubbed them fiercely against the sheets. She began to imagine that he'd actually *held* her, that he'd been reluctant to let her go and that she'd actually had to *drag* herself away from him!

At last she fell asleep, and he followed her into the house of dreams. Only now he looked dreadfully sad as if he was reproaching her for having fled from him and leaving him in so grim and lonely a place as a coffin.

'No – no – no!' she wept. 'Go away from me, please!' But he would not; he came to her each night, with his sad, grave smile and his pale hands extended as if for a grave embrace. So gentle did he seem, that she lost all fear of him, and by the end of a week Miss Jessop was hopelessly, despairingly in love with Orlando Brown. Never was there a stranger love awakened in a young girl's breast; it was a love that could neither live nor change nor die.

On the first anniversary of his funeral, among the many tokens of loving remembrance that were laid upon the grave under the elder tree in St Martin's Church-yard, appeared a wreath of flowering ivy and wild garlic, bearing a black-edged card on which was written – rather badly – 'Be my vallintyne.'

However, by the second anniversary, both the writing and the spelling had improved, for Jessop & Potters-field's were still prosperous enough to afford a tutor for their daughter.

'Be my valentine,' pleaded the card in the ivy wreath to the youth who slumbered below.

Then, that very year, Hawkins was taken on by Alfred Todds's and Jessop & Pottersfield's fortunes began to decline.

Mr Jessop's solemn countenance, long dignified by

the custom of loss, became a little frayed at the edges by the loss of custom. He took to fault-finding, particularly with his daughter, whose reluctance to enter wholeheartedly into the trade had not escaped him. But Miss Jessop, anxious to lay the blame where it really belonged, tossed her head and declared:

'If only it had been that Hawkins who'd passed away instead of some others I could mention. *That's* a funeral I'd have been happy to furnish, pa! Not that,' she went on, '*we* would have buried him! More a job for a gardener, I'd say!'

'Go to your room, miss!'

'I'm not a child, pa. If I go to my room, it will be because I choose to.'

She went; after all, there was always Orlando Brown. She was now fourteen and catching up with the dead youth fast. When first they'd met, so to speak, in the front parlour, he'd been a quiet and serious sixteen, and she a timid, childish eleven. The gap between them had

seemed enormous. But now it had narrowed and they were almost on a footing.

This strange circumstance both frightened and fascinated her and she couldn't help wondering how she would feel when they were both the same age? Would her love suddenly become mature? There was no doubt that, as time passed, she felt her affection growing deeper and more settled. He was such a comfort and he was always *there*, waiting for her. Everything else might change, but he was constant. Not so much as by the flicker of an eyelid did he alter from that first wild vision of him. He was . . . eternal.

Which was more than could be said for Hawkins. When she, Miss Jessop, was fifteen and looking like a lily opening, Messrs Todds's apprentice was already seventeen and ageing as noticeably as a leaf in autumn. Withering, one might almost say. In a year or two, he'd be an old man, while Orlando Brown would still be a smiling sixteen, smooth as candle wax!

Sixteen! It seemed impossible; and yet it must come. How would she feel about Orlando Brown who'd once seemed so unattainable?

At last the miracle happened. She was sixteen, and he was sixteen – still. It was as if he'd paused to wait for her, had held back time itself. She imagined him to be standing at the end of a corridor of months and years, with his fine transparent hands outstretched, watching her through closed eyes and smiling his grave smile as she stumbled on towards him, forever catching her hastening feet against the sharp stones of childhood. She blushed as she remembered grubby bandages round barked shins and grazed knees . . .

'Be my valentine,' she inscribed with loving care on the back of one of her pa's trade cards, and pinned it in the middle of the ivy wreath.

On the bright cold morning of February 14th, she hastened to St Martin's Churchyard with the strangest of forebodings. She knew that something must happen to her, but she could not say what. Although one part of her knew that her dream-life was no more than an idle phantom, another, deeper part kept urging upon her a sense of terrified expectation. Was this day to be an end – or a beginning?

Reason told her that Orlando Brown, waiting in the corridor of time, must inevitably dwindle into yesterday as she passed him by; but her heart cried out fiercely that this must not be so.

As she entered the precincts of the cemetery, St Valentine's sun peered over the tops of the neighbouring roofs and strewed all the grass with long shadows. All the headstones seemed to be wearing black streamers, as if a great concourse of mutes had laid their stone hats on the ground and gone off into the bushes and behind the yew trees for a quiet repast.

Miss Jessop, deeply veiled in fresh black muslin, walked uncertainly across the grass towards the grave beneath the elder tree. Although she was alone in the churchyard, she felt that eyes were watching her from everywhere. The feeling was so strong that she had to pause and gather up her courage. It was, as nearly as she could remember, exactly the feeling she'd had as she'd

pushed open the door of the front parlour at home, so long ago. Were the same eyes watching on this day of days?

She reached the grave and looked up at the over-hanging bough of the elder tree. Was there some mysterious emanation of him, drawn up by the tree's roots and dwelling in the knotted wood itself?

She knelt down and laid the wreath against the beloved stone.

'Be my valentine!' she breathed to the grass. 'Oh my dearest darling, you've waited for me so long! Never let me pass you by . . . please!'

Tears flooded her eyes as reason – hateful, horrible reason! – told her that she *must* go on and leave the youth behind. He was rooted to his place as surely as the elder tree was rooted in his heart. From this day forward she could only look back and look back; and each time she turned, he would have dwindled a little more until at last he would have disappeared altogether.

Then the winds would blow cold across her; they would shake her limbs and break her bloom till the sixteen-year-old Orlando Brown would never even have recognized her . . .

She stood up. She'd lingered long enough. She knew she must go back to Little Knightrider Street and to the quarrelsome misery of a home growing poorer by the week and day. Then she would have to go out again to Shoemaker's Row where old Mrs Noades was dying. She would have to accost the physician, beg a word with the servants, watch with straining eyes for the drawing of a blind . . . and pray that Hawkins didn't get there before her.

If only one could leave a card without causing

offence! But that was impossible. What a vile trade it was in which ordinary businesslike prudence – such as anyone might employ – earned you nothing but horror and contempt! A sweep – a common chimney-sweep – might call upon a house in high summer and offer to sweep the chimneys before the winter's need of fires. But should an undertaker knock up a house and offer his services perhaps no more than a single day in advance, he'd be kicked down the stairs like a dog!

She left the grave and drifted silently across the grass. She could still feel eyes upon her, eyes filled with longing and regret. Even so, she must not look back; reason told her it would be madness . . .

She came to the lych gate. Surely, after all these years, she and he were entitled to one last look upon each other? Just one brief look—?

She turned. She saw the grave. Her heart leaped and danced! The wreath had gone!

She shut her eyes tightly and turned away. She'd made a mistake, of course. The wreath *must* have been

there – most likely it had slipped down onto the grass. That was it! Her eyes had deceived her.

Reason bade her look again; but this time her heart was adamant. She could not bear to look again and destroy the sudden wild thought that somehow *he* had risen to claim his tribute.

She returned home with scarcely an idea of how she had found her way. Her eyes were shining like stars. Mr Jessop, however, was not disposed to take this into account when he berated his daughter for her absence.

It seemed that old Mrs Noades had passed away and Todds's were furnishing. It was no trifling affair. The Noades's were a large family with many friends. Was Miss Jessop aware that it meant half a gross of pair black shammy gloves, the same of mourning rings, white hatbands – to say nothing of crêpe, silk and best scarves and hoods at ninepence apiece?

'Thanks to your dreamy negligence, miss, we have now lost upwards of three hundred pounds! I hope you are satisfied!'

'You hate me! I know you hate me!' cried Miss Jessop, who could think of no other defence; and she rushed from the house in a storm of sobs and tears.

'Everybody hates me!' she panted, whirling through the streets like a wind-blown black bloom. 'Everybody except – *him*!'

She rushed towards the churchyard. She had to go to him. She'd always known that this day would have to be fatal to one of them. Now she understood that he and she must be together for ever. The vanishing of her wreath had been a sign that he accepted her.

But how was it to come about? Various fearful thoughts intruded upon her. She thought of the bough

of the elder tree; then she thought of twisting up her veil into a thin black rope and hanging herself above his grave. They'd find her, swinging like a broken blossom, and then they'd be sorry!

She reached the churchyard and gazed towards the grave that was so soon to be her own.

'No – no!' she cried. 'It cannot be!'

The wreath was still there. Either her eyes had deceived her, or even *he* had turned away from her.

With bowed head she trudged towards the grave, even though there seemed little point, now, in hanging herself over someone who had, after all, ignored her tribute.

Mournfully she stared at the wreath propped up against the headstone. Her eyes widened and she caught in her breath. It was not the same wreath! In place of ivy and wild garlic, was now an offering of dark holly, speckled with berries, bright as blood!

And the card? Even that was changed. Now it read: 'I will be your valentine.'

'Orlando – Orlando Brown!' she cried; and tears rushed from her eyes and caught in her veil where they sparkled like dew on a web. 'I *will* be your valentine!'

With shaking hands she took off her veil and began to twist it fiercely, pulling at it every now and then to make sure it would be strong enough to bear her weight.

Now she stood upon tiptoe and secured the black cord she'd made to the bough of the elder tree. She dragged on it several times; and the whole tree shook with grief. She began to make a noose . . .

'Miss Jessop – Miss Jessop!'

She released the cord and whirled round. Wild love and despair gave way to indignation and fury. Hawkins was standing there! Odious, horrible Hawkins, glossy as a slug in a new suit of blacks. Even his boots shone like coffin handles. He looked more got up to kill than to bury!

What did he want? Sincerest condolences, miss, and might we have the honour of furnishing your funeral? Ugh! One couldn't even hang oneself without Hawkins getting the trade for Todds's!

'Wh— what are you doing here, Mr Hawkins?' She could feel herself shaking all over with anger.

'I – er – was just visiting, Miss Jessop.'

The smartly dressed undertaker's apprentice was quite taken aback by Miss Jessop's annoyance. If there'd been words on the tip of his tongue, he seemed unable to shake them free. He looked unprofessionally dismayed . . .

Miss Jessop, seeing this, pushed home her advantage by declaring that it was a pity he was just visiting and hadn't come to stay. She made her meaning as plain as she could by glancing across the sunswept garden of graves and scraping the grass with her own neat black shoe.

For a moment Hawkins's dreamy eyes flickered angrily; then he compressed his lips and sighed. The undertaker's apprentice and the undertaker's daughter stood silently, breathing deeply.

'I'm sure, Miss Jessop,' said Hawkins, relaxing into a rueful smile, 'that were I to come here to stay, your pa – Mr Jessop – would furnish the occasion 'andsomely.'

'Nothing would give us greater pleasure, Mr Hawkins.'

'Likewise for you, Miss Jessop. We – Todds's – would leave no stone unturned to inter you like a queen. White 'atbands and shammy gloves all round. Though in honest truth, I'd sooner such a piece of business went to your house before ever coming to ours.'

Miss Jessop scowled as she unravelled Hawkins's gallantry which had been delivered with solemn charm.

'Friend of yours, Miss Jessop?' murmured Hawkins, nodding down towards the grave beside which they stood. His eyes lingered on the wreath. 'A dear departed, was he? Taken when 'e was sixteen. That's a year less than me . . . He's grassed over well; but then it's five years and the soil's good in St Martin's . . .'

Hastily Miss Jessop looked away. Something black was flickering out of the corner of her eye. With a start she realized it was the veil from which she'd meant to hang herself. It was still tied to the bough of the elder tree.

'I – I never knew him,' said Miss Jessop awkwardly.

'It was just an occasion we – we furnished . . . a long time ago. It's no more than that.'

'Yes, miss. As you say. Only I supposed—' (he indicated the twisted veil) 'that it was a favour, a love-ribbon, in a manner of speaking . . . like round a mute's wand. I thought to myself, that's a beautiful, poetic idea . . . making mutes of the trees. I was going to ask you if we – Todds's – might adopt it . . . that is, wherever there's a suitable branch, of course! I hope, Miss Jessop, you wouldn't take it amiss if we – Todds's – was to do something in the same line? We could call them Jessops, if you like . . . ?'

All Miss Jessop's anger returned with a rush. It was intolerable that the insufferable Hawkins should turn even the evidence of her despair to his own business advantage. She didn't want to look at him. She reached up to untie her veil which had become ridiculous and humiliating in her eyes. Hawkins, unaware of her feelings, came courteously to her assistance. He smelled of varnish and aromatic herbs and his nose was as smooth as marble.

Briefly his hand touched hers over the knot in the veil. Miss Jessop snatched away in instinctive horror, remembering other hands she'd touched. She felt she'd betrayed the sleeper under the grass, who lay so quietly, listening and watching . . .

Surreptitiously she wiped her fingers clean as Hawkins untied the knot, smoothed out the delicate muslin and returned it to her.

'It's a nice stone, Miss Jessop,' said Hawkins, looking down at the grave again. 'They don't do them like that any more. They never do the inscription as deep. Sometimes it's not much more than a scratch.'

'Mr Jessop has always been very particular about the stone.'

'And well known for it,' said Hawkins gravely. 'Even Mr Todds used to say that when his time came he'd as soon Jessop & Pottersfield's furnished him as anyone else in the trade.'

'Really?' said Miss Jessop, taken off guard and warmed by the unusual tribute from a rival. 'Did he really say that?'

'Oh yes indeed!' said Hawkins eagerly. 'Good taste, he always said. That's what Jessop & Pottersfield's have. Impeccable taste. Do you know, in the old days—'

'Yes! In the old days!' interrupted Miss Jessop bitterly. 'But things are very different now! We've not furnished anybody for a month, Mr Hawkins! A whole month! Did you know that? Of course you did! But can you know what it means to *us*, Mr Hawkins?'

Hawkins looked momentarily guilty and distraught; then with an impulsive gesture, he clasped Miss Jessop's hands.

'Things will look up, Miss Jessop! Please don't you worry! Everything will be all right! It – it's only the season. Come March and a cold snap and before you can say "dust to dust" there'll be bereavements and funerals left over and to spare! Mark my words, Miss Jessop, you'll not be able to move in the shops for coffins and hat-bands and shammy gloves! Oh, the good times are coming back, Miss Jessop!'

'Are you sure of it, Mr Hawkins?' asked Miss Jessop, undeniably touched by the stately youth's concern for her.

'As sure as we're both standing here in the church-yard!' cried Hawkins, clasping Miss Jessop's hands even more tightly. Gently she freed herself and Hawkins took off his shining black hat to reveal a pale brow, bright with perspiration.

He closed his eyes and tendered his sincerest apologies for having taken such liberties with Miss Jessop. He did not wish her to think him lacking in sympathy or respect; it was just that he had been borne away by the sight of her distress . . .

She accepted his apology and Hawkins, with immense relief and dignity, proposed a stroll among the sunny tombstones to refresh them both. So they walked, side by side – the funereal youth and the funereal girl – pausing by stones and monuments and sombre urns, criticizing this and admiring that; for it was their trade.

Many of the sleepers had been laid to rest by Jessop & Pottersfield; Miss Jessop remembered them all and talked of the lively times of her pa's heyday. She found herself recollecting the old mutes of her childhood – tall,

sad fellows decked with crêpe weepers like melancholy maypoles – who'd made her laugh with strange jokes when she'd cried over a dead mouse or a broken doll. . .

They read the inscriptions as if turning the pages of an old stone album: 'Deeply loved . . . deeply missed . . . we will be together again . . . loving . . . loving . . .' Love was everywhere, and the crisp grass rustled and sighed.

'Is this one of yours, miss?' asked Hawkins, pausing beside a simple grey headstone that marked a newly grassed grave. Miss Jessop shook her head.

'Samuel Bold,' read out Hawkins. 'Lamplighter late of Cripplegate Ward. *To them which sat in the shadow of death, LIGHT is sprung up.*'

'Very suitable,' said Miss Jessop.

'If I'd furnished 'im,' said Hawkins softly, 'I'd 'ave advised a monument, Miss Jessop.'

'What sort of a monument, Mr Hawkins . . . bearing in mind the circumstances of the bereaved?'

'An angel, Miss Jessop. A boy angel, holdin' a torch. Might I show you, Miss Jessop?'

She nodded, and the undertaker's apprentice, with graceful decorum, laid a white handkerchief with a black border at the foot of the grave. Then, placing his hat beside him, he knelt.

At first, Miss Jessop was inclined to smile . . . until she saw it was no smiling matter. The youth, upon one knee, had lifted up his arms and was holding them out towards her. His long fingers trembled and on his face was an expression that would have melted the finest Aberdeen granite. Beloved . . . loving . . . dear one was carved all over it till there was no room left to end it even with a date.

'Would you – would you care for a monument like this?'

'Mr Hawkins!'

'Please, Miss Jessop! Tell me—'

'I – I don't know . . . I can't say . . . You must get up, Mr Hawkins . . . The grass is chilly and damp. You will catch cold . . . your death of cold . . .'

'And if I did, would you put such a monument over me?'

'I don't know – I don't know! B-besides, Todds's would – would be furnishing you . . . I'm sure they would! And – and in any case, Mr Hawkins, you wouldn't look half so fine in stone!'

'I love you, Miss Jessop! I've always loved you,' whispered the youth, his eyes shining and his face pale with hope.

'Please don't say such things, Mr Hawkins! You can't mean them...'

But he assured her that he did. Still kneeling, he went on to tell her how, when he first came into the trade, he'd admired her, longed for her and dreamed of her. He told her, shyly, of how, in the early days, he'd carved her name on every coffin lid and scratched it on headstones where none but he could see it. He told her how he'd vowed to make himself worthy of her. He'd prayed for strength to work and work to make something of himself so that he could approach her. Every funeral he helped to furnish had been a step nearer...

'Oh stop, stop!' sobbed Miss Jessop. She was immeasurably distressed and ashamed to hear that all Hawkins's industry, that had ruined her family, had been only for her.

'Everything has been for you,' said Hawkins, rising to his feet and standing so close to her that she felt dizzy from the smell of varnish and herbs.

'And now,' he murmured into her ear, 'the time 'as come, Miss Jessop.'

He went on to tell her, with mingled modesty and pride, that Todds's were opening up in Queen Street and that he, Hawkins, was to manage.

'Though I'm still only a 'prentice, miss, Mr Todds 'as promised me the management. He only told me yesterday, Miss Jessop... and my 'eart sang like a nightingale. I knew my St Valentine's Day 'ad come round at last. That's why I came here, to find you...'

'You came here for me?'

Miss Jessop trembled and blushed deeply as she recollected what she'd been doing when Hawkins had found her ... the dreadful preparations she'd been making.

'I – wasn't going to ... really ... I wasn't ...' she stammered, clutching her veil and wishing it would vanish away.

Hawkins smiled and shook his head. A natural compassion for distress prevented him from telling her how panic-stricken he'd been as he'd watched her about to make away with herself. Suddenly his smile broadened as he realized how his impulsive saving of Miss Jessop's life had deprived the new premises of a client. Mr Todds would not have been pleased with him ...

'Why are you smiling, Mr Hawkins?'

'Pleasure, Miss Jessop, at being with you.'

She accepted his explanation even though she felt it to be not entirely true. The undertaker's apprentice bent to pick up his hat and his black-edged handkerchief. He asked if Miss Jessop would honour him by visiting the new premises? It was very close, he assured her; no more than a walking funeral off ...

He extended his arm to Miss Jessop and together they strolled from the lamplighter's grave.

'We're opening up day after tomorrow, Miss Jessop. With old Mrs Noades.'

She bit her lip with a sudden pang of envy.

'We're making a real occasion of it,' went on Hawkins proudly. 'We're donating ten yards of black silk to the church at our own expense. There'll be four mutes with white 'atbands and weepers on their wands done up with black love-ribbons. Six branch boys with real wax candles and shammy gloves all round – even for the servants. No 'orses, of course as she'll be going from Queen Street, but there'll be a featherman ...'

'What's that, Mr Hawkins?'

'Ah! It's the newest thing. French and very smart. It's a tray of black ostrich plumes carried on the feather-man's 'ead. Works out at two shillings . . .'

'It sounds very handsome—'

'Would you care to see it, Miss Jessop? If you are not otherwise engaged, would you attend the occasion as my guest? It would be a great compliment and I can't think of anything that would set off a furnishing to better advantage than your presence, Miss Jessop!'

'Why, thank you, Mr Hawkins.'

'The repast is to be at The Eagle and Child, on the river.'

Miss Jessop inclined her head.

'In the old days, Mr Hawkins, we used to have little honey cakes in black paper cups. They made a very good impression . . .'

'I'll order them directly!'

They paused by the lych gate.

'I told you,' said Hawkins, so softly that she could scarcely hear him, 'that I love you, Miss Jessop and that, for me, the time 'as come.'

He put his hand upon hers where it lay in the crook of his smooth black elbow like a bouquet of lilies.

'In two years I'll be out of my apprenticeship and will be of a man's estate . . .'

She began to tremble violently; her heart fluttered and she could only draw breath with difficulty. She knew he was about to make her an offer . . . that he was on the point of asking her to become Mrs Hawkins.

Her mind, confused by the profoundest agitation, struggled for words to reject the youth. She had no choice but to reject him. Her heart was already given; and how could she, in the twinkling of an eye, turn from hanging herself for a dead love to accepting the advances of a brand-new live one? It was too much to ask! She could never, never be wife to one who had never been her valentine. There had to be a springtime of love before its summer. And besides—

'Will you – will you accept my sincerest affection and become my wife?' breathed the funereal lover in tones that would have done credit to a parson.

Alas, poor Hawkins! He was too conscientious an apprentice to quite cast off the quality of his trade! Decorum and respect were instinctive to him in the presence of an occasion; and what greater occasion had he ever faced than this present one of declaring his lifelong love?

'Will you marry me?' he repeated, bowing his head.

Miss Jessop, no less conscious of decorum and respect

– and admiring them in their proper place – turned her
head away and gazed, with anguish and pleading,
towards the grave under the elder tree. If only *he* could
help her . . . if only *he* could send her a sign!

Her eyes widened. The wreath – his wreath – had
gone! What did it mean? . . .

'Will you be Mrs 'awkins?'

'The wreath . . . it – it's gone!'

Hawkins, somewhat dismayed by this reception of his
addresses, followed the direction of Miss Jessop's gaze.
He frowned; he scowled; he muttered something under
his breath. With an unaccustomed agitation he freed
her arm from his.

'It's not gone far,' he said; and began to walk, at first
slowly and reverently among the headstones, ap-
parently bowing to each loving memory as he passed.

Suddenly there was a quicker movement among the

tombs. Something small and earthy scuttled out. It might have been a large rat. Then it squealed: 'Look out! 'e's arter us!'

Two similar creatures emerged from concealment and began to fly, with screams and shrieks, before the advancing figure that, they sensed, was bent upon vengeance.

Hawkins's pace quickened; he broke into a long-legged, dancing run. His hat tumbled off and his fair hair flew out like an unquenched candle. The demon children squealed with terrified delight and went zigzag among the dead. Hawkins, with coat tails flying, leaped the graves, swung on the iron railings that en-

closed the monuments and vaulted the 'loving memories' and 'deeply beloveds' as lightly as a bird.

Miss Jessop, standing by the lych gate, looked on, half in terror and half in hapless fascination as life sprang up among the meek and helpless dead; how it danced and scampered, squealed and shouted and became, at length, a wild, fantastic game in which the silent sleepers under the grass played the only part they could – by offering their 'loving memories' as obstacles, concealments, refuges and, ultimately, stepping-stones for the triumph of—

He'd caught them! He'd stalked them round a black marble monument to the memory of a clockmaker and his wife, and trapped them against the railings! Miss Jessop heard his shout of triumph and the children's wail of dismay. What would he do with them? Nothing.

He laughed and let them go. Wrath and sternness were no part of Hawkins . . .

He returned to Miss Jessop, panting and bearing the now battered circlet of holly.

'Here!' he said. 'They nicked it. They nicked yours, too, earlier on. They brought it to me in the shop. I paid them and – and put this one in its place.'

'And – and the card?' murmured Miss Jessop, overcome with remorse and confusion. 'Did you put that there?'

'You read it, then?'

She nodded.

'Will you be my valentine?' asked Hawkins, flushed and weary from his wild pursuit. 'Will you, my love?'

'Yes,' said Miss Jessop, who could not find, either in her mind or in her heart, the words to reject him. 'I will be your valentine!'

They walked from the lych gate and left the churchyard behind them. They strolled into Queen Street to view the new premises, twined in each other's arms. People smiled as they passed, and an old lamplighter, dragging his ladder, recollected that it was St Valentine's Day and, remembering an ancient custom, mumbled:

'There they goes; the ivy girl and the holly boy.'

# Labour in Vain

*to Daisy and John*

'My ma,' said Gully to his friends, 'looks after our family leather business. In quite a big way, y'know. Old-established premises in one of them quiet parts off Old Change.'

He himself was apprenticed to Noades's, the buckle-makers in Shoemakers Row, where he worked in brass, plate and pinchbeck with chips of Bristol stone sparingly cemented into the more fancy styles.

'My son,' confided Mrs Gully to a new neighbour, 'works in the jewellery line. 'andles pearls and diamonds as if they was as common as them black beads you're wearin'. Meanin' no offence, of course . . .'

She lived in Labour-in-Vain Yard, where, with the help of an ancient journeyman, she kept a small, dark cobbler's shop that always reeked of leather and feet.

'I once worked for a lady what had a real diamond brooch,' murmured the neighbour, forlornly fingering her beads. 'It was in—'

'My Gully don't go all that much on diamonds,' interrupted Mrs Gully, raising her voice as the journeyman started hammering in the workroom next door. ' 'e thinks they're a bit common nowadays.'

'She used to wash it in buttermilk!' shouted the neighbour anxiously.

'Sometimes 'e's brung me things on Motherin' Sunday,' howled Mrs Gully, 'that wouldn't disgrace 'anover Square!'

'The lady what I worked for lived in—'

'The Lord God Almighty,' bellowed Mrs Gully, when the journeyman's hammering stopped, leaving her voice exposed as a raw, passionate shriek, 'knows what 'e'll bring me next!'

They were a proud dynasty, were the Gullys, and rising in pride with every generation. But this same pride, which might have united them, divided them in the cruellest way. Although, as the crow flies, it was less than half a mile from Shoemakers Row to Labour-in-Vain Yard, as the proud apprentice walked it might as well have been a thousand. Gully visited his ma scarcely one Sunday in a month; and even when he did, it was with feelings of awkwardness and distress.

Being in the buckle business, which, by its very nature, was some inches off the ground, he felt himself removed from the odious trade of feet entirely. He didn't care to think of it at all; and particularly he

didn't like to dwell, in his mind, upon his ma's dingy workroom where the old journeyman sat with his bunioned toes exposed and stinking like the old soles he patched.

So he covered it up in his heart and referred to 'the family leather business', in tones of immense refinement. In consequence of this, he couldn't help feeling angry and bitter whenever he called and saw that his ma was making a liar of him.

Similarly Mrs Gully resented her son, not because of *his* pride, but because of her own. Having represented him as being in the jewellery line, she was offended that he never brought her the gifts that would have been proper to that exalted trade.

Nevertheless, she felt a certain regret, and, with the approach of each Mothering Sunday, she felt a warmth coming on and made sundry vows to herself that, this time 'things would go better'.

' 'e'll be comin' tomorrer of course,' said Mrs Gully, with a sudden rush of gentleness that encouraged the new neighbour.

'The lady what I worked for—'

Then the hammering started up again and Mrs Gully had to shout.

'Tomorrer! My son! For tea!'

'Tomorrer!' swore Gully to himself as he stalked along Shoemakers Row on the Saturday morning. 'Tomorrer I'll reely try to make things go with a swing!' He, too, couldn't help feeling sorrow for the rift between himself and his ma.

'Yes,' he murmured, as he turned down Puddle Dock Hill in order to avoid passing too close to Labour-in-Vain Yard, 'tomorrer I'll reely go out of me way!'

He was on an errand to Janner's of Trig Lane to buy some silver thread and was dressed in his best clothes and wearing his new black shammy gloves. They'd been given to him (together with a black silk hatband which he'd given to his ma) last month when he'd gone to old Mrs Noades's funeral, and every time he put them on, he thought of deaths of mothers and resolved, before it was too late, to heal the breach with his own.

For this good intention he'd even bought her something – something he knew she'd like. Every year, on the Friday before Mothering Sunday, Mr Noades put up a notice in the workroom reminding everyone of the custom of taking gifts to their mothers and offering, at greatly reduced prices, various items of stock that had been hanging fire on the shelves. Gully, at considerable expense, had bought a pair of pinchbeck buckles ornamented with brilliants that, in the gloom of the cobbler's shop, could have passed as gold and diamonds. They'd been made up into the initial of a lady who'd never come back to claim them; and although they were plainly Ds, Gully felt that it was not beyond human ingenuity to represent them as an elegant form of Gs.

'Tomorrer,' he repeated as he turned into Trig Lane, 'things will reely be good!' He thrust his hand in his pocket to feel the sharp little parcel, and he smiled so that his plain, small-eyed face looked almost handsome.

He was still smiling when he stopped outside the silver thread spinners.

'Went to Janner's, yesterday, ma,' he rehearsed to himself, knowing how she liked to hear about the noble metals. 'You know . . . in the precious line. Gold an' silver 'eaped up with no more regard than you'd 'ave for old boots!'

He went into the shop and stood politely before the trade counter.

'Six ounces of silver thread for Mr Noades's of Shoe-makers, miss.'

It was Miss Janner herself who greeted him. She did not look pleased. She had been told to work on this Saturday morning and she was nursing a strong sense of injury. She compressed her lips and sniffed.

'You can go and ask my pa. First floor. Workroom. I'm not a servant in this house.'

Gully went, feeling in his present mood not a little shocked by this sample of a child's pride.

He climbed the stairs and, reaching the workroom door, knocked. There was no reply so he knocked again and began to turn the handle.

'Come in quick and shut that murdering door!' shouted an angry voice. 'Before you blow me bankrupt!'

The workroom was tremendously long and low, extending the whole width of the house. At one end it was lit by a window and at the other by the red, watchful eye of a fire.

Nor was the fire the only watchful thing. Mr Janner himself – a bulky, long-limbed person – stood in the middle of the room with a look that crawled unceasingly along the shimmering threads that were stretched between the spindle women by the window and the silver women by the fire. His was the voice that had greeted Gully; but after one hasty glance, he paid no further attention to him. His eyes returned, with a mixture of hunger and dread, to their previous scrutiny.

As the spindle women turned their wheels and drew

the valuable thread towards them, he sucked in his lips warningly; and as the silver women at the other end of the room paid out their silk, deftly binding it with wisps of silver as fine as hair as it passed through their palms, he blew out his lips menacingly as if to say:

'Watch it! Watch it! I know you're trying to nick me silver; but just you try it! That's all – just you try it!'

Gully stood stock still. The atmosphere of suspicion, watchfulness and value in the long room was the most solemn thing he had ever known; he was in the presence of many hundreds of pounds. It was another world. He struggled in his mind to come to terms with it and find the words that would conjure it up for the pleasure of his ma in Labour-in-Vain Yard.

But it was quite beyond him and, try as he might, the only image that came into his head was the eerie,

slightly unpleasant one that Mr Janner looked like an enormous spider in the midst of the silver strands, brooding hungrily on the seven or eight pitiful female flies that were trapped in the suburbs of his web.

'What is it, lad?'

'Six ounces of silver thread for Mr Noades's of Shoemakers, if you please, sir. The lady downstairs—'

'I know.'

Mr Janner frowned and nodded, then left his web by way of holding down the threads and climbing over them with his long, flexible legs – which made him look more like a spider than ever. He had very small feet and wore buckles that, by daylight looked brass and by firelight, gold.

He went to a shelf while the threads continued on their ceaseless, quivering journey from the light of the fire to the light of day. A vague sensation of easing and murmuring sprang up at either end of the travelling threads.

'I'm watching you,' said Mr Janner, beaming round suddenly at the spinners. 'I'm still watching you, ladies!'

He beckoned to Gully.

'Here, lad. Come over here and take a look at the back of me head.'

Gully obliged.

'Now – you tell them ladies what you can see.'

'I—' began Gully.

'That's it!' cried Mr Janner triumphantly. 'Eyes! Eyes in the back of me head! So watch out, ladies! Just because I turn me back, it don't mean I can't see you!'

Then he murmured to Gully:

'Watch 'em for me, lad. Make sure they don't wet their hands!'

With this curious injunction, Mr Janner turned his back and, visibly trembling with anxiety, lifted down a spindle and began to weigh out the precious thread.

'Don't take your eyes off 'em, lad,' he muttered. 'Watch what they do with their hands. It's all right if they warm 'em ... to keep 'em dry ... but nothing more than that. There's eyes on you, ladies!' he shouted out. 'There's eyes everywhere!'

Obediently, and with a sense of the trust put in him, Gully watched the spinners as, with dull faces and incredibly rapid fingers, they continued their glittering toil. Then once again an eerie image drifted into his head and he couldn't help thinking how strange it was that flies should be set to spinning the spider's web for him.

Little by little, as he watched – for Mr Janner was taking his time and weighing was a tedious business – he found his gaze drifting helplessly from hands to faces, and to one face in particular till it was fixed upon it to the exclusion of everything else.

It was the face of the girl who stood closest to the fire; and such was the illumination that she seemed like a flame herself; her hair was reddish and her eyes flared and sparkled as she turned her head.

Then, suddenly, one of these little blazes seemed to be put out as she winked at Gully. Eagerly he winked back. She smiled; and he smiled back. She blew him a quick, secret kiss; and he blew one back.

On the way out of the workroom, after his business was concluded, he managed to linger by her.

'When d'you finish?'

'Dark.'
'Doin' anything tonight?'
'Maybe.'
'Meet me outside?'
'Maybe.'
'Go on!'
'All right, then. Outside – at dark.'

The kiss! Gully couldn't get over it. It had happened so suddenly: the raised hand, the lowered face, the pursed lips, the quick, fiery smile – and then, puff! Though it had been lighter than the wisps of silver that rustled through the girl's hands, it had struck Gully with the force of a cannonball and blown a hole through his head and heart.

He was fifteen and she was fifteen and she was his first real girl. He went back to Shoemakers Row like a lad apprenticed to the trade of sky and stars.

'I thought you mightn't come,' she said. She'd been waiting for him in windy Trig Lane, with a wild yellow cloak blowing all round her as if she'd brought an unwilling friend. She looked agitated.

'And there was me thinkin' *you* mightn't,' said Gully, which really didn't do justice to the heart-aching fears and doubts he'd gone through during the long afternoon.

'I *said* I'd come, didn't I?'

'So did I.'

They began to walk down towards the river. She told him her name was Daisy LaSalle . . .

'That's French, ain't it?' a shade uneasily. Anything French he knew was costly, and the buckles he'd bought his ma had left him in reduced circumstances.

'From Spitalfields, where the weavers live,' explained Miss LaSalle. 'You know, them huge knots.'

Gully, not knowing that this was Miss LaSalle's effort at 'Huguenots', nodded in a baffled fashion.

'Me ma was an actress.'

'I s'pose it was your pa what was in the rope business,' said Gully, dimly pursuing the notion of knots.

It turned out that Miss LaSalle wasn't any too sure about her pa. So far as she knew, he'd been either a beadle or a lamplighter from Bishopsgate who'd been very sweet on her ma and had told her he'd never lit lamps half as bright as her eyes.

'I expect it was 'im,' said Gully; and meant it. Miss LaSalle really looked luminous in the dark March night. Gully could have walked by the light of her anywhere.

'Where are we going?'

'I thought we might 'ave a bite of supper at The Three Cranes.'

'I don't want you to spend all your money on me,' said Miss LaSalle, giving his arm a quick squeeze and, at the same time, bestowing on him a nervous smile.

'That's all right,' said Gully, and went on to explain that, although he was only Mr Noades's apprentice, his ma looked after the family leather business and was in quite a big way . . .

'Making shoes?'

'N— not reely,' said Gully, thinking of the ancient journeyman and his shameful trade. 'We don't 'ave much to do with – with feet.'

Miss LaSalle gave his arm another squeeze, and Gully, over the worst, went on to say that his ma didn't actually work herself, but looked after the staff.

'They've been with 'er a long time, of course. It's a real family trade. Old-established, y'know . . . in one of them quiet parts off Old Change.'

They came to Trig Stairs from where Gully insisted they took a waterman's boat to The Three Cranes. A friend of his – a clockmaker's apprentice from Carter Lane whom he'd consulted – had advised this. He always did it himself when he'd got a new girl and he wasn't sure if the game would turn out to be worth the candle. The river unsettled their stomachs so they didn't want to eat much.

Under the influence of the wind, the water turned out to be choppy enough to slice onions. They both started off cheerfully enough, with Gully waxing expansive about his ma's circumstances, when, after a dozen black and awful yards, he found he had to shut his mouth to stop everything inside him coming up and flying out. By the time they reached The Three Cranes, Miss LaSalle had to help him disembark and, to his dazed

shame, pay the waterman herself as he was too ill to do more than moan.

The landlady found them a table in a corner, removed from all sight of the river.

'Brandy and port wine,' she said, eyeing Gully sympathetically. 'That'll settle his stomach. Just half a pint taken straight off; then he'll be fit and ready for mutton chops and kisses for afters, eh?'

She proved only partly right. He drank down the potion and, sure enough, he fancied kisses for afters, and made several attempts to claim them; but he couldn't quite manage to keep down the mutton chops. Repeatedly he slumped back in his corner; he was a much divided apprentice: his heart was in the right place, but his stomach was most definitely not.

Nonetheless, as long as he stayed perfectly still and didn't breathe too heavily, he felt quite well. He was with his girl and she was shining in front of him like all the lamps in the Strand. Carefully he told her over and over again about his ma, as, somehow, she seemed interested and he felt it peculiarly important for her to know.

'We're reely in a big way, y'know . . . leather an' all that . . .'

'I suppose you'll be taking it over when – when your ma gets too old? You'll be following in your pa's footsteps . . .'

'I thought I told you,' said Gully carefully, 'that we don't 'ave all that much to do with feet.'

They left The Three Cranes at ten o'clock, and walked arm in arm along the river, back towards Trig Lane. Gully was feeling much, much better. The worst of his experience was over and he felt only a little light-headed. He assured Miss LaSalle that there was no need for her to walk nearest the river as he was in no danger of falling in. He was, he said, as steady as anything . . .

Just to prove it, he managed to kiss Miss LaSalle three times; but on the third occasion he was dismayed to feel that her cheek was salty and wet with tears.

'I – I ain't 'urt you?' he asked anxiously.

'No – no. Not really.'

'Was I 'oldin' on to your arm too tight?'

'N— no. It wasn't that.'

'Was it – was it the mutton chops and . . . and all that?'

' 'course not!'

'Was it – was it me kissin' you so soon?'

' 'course not!'

'Then what is it? I ain't done nothing else!'

'It's just that I lost me place. At Janner's. I've been turned off.'

'Was it on account of me? Was it because I talked to you?'

'Not really. It was . . . that kiss I blew you. He saw me. I'll swear he's really got eyes in the back of his head! He saw it. He shouted and swore I'd licked me hand. Came up and felt it just after you'd gone. It was wet all right. I was sweatin' with fright!'

'But what was wrong in that?'

'Wet hands. It's a trick of the trade. That's why we got the fire . . . to keep drying ourselves off. If your hands are wet, you can damp the silk and make it weigh right. Then you can nick his silver and no one finds out till it's too late. But there's not much chance at Janner's. He's that careful he won't drink a drop all day, 'case he has to go out for a pee. He'll die in that there silver harness of his . . . and his last words will be: "I'm a-watching you, ladies!" That's why he's in such a big way . . .'

Gully stood as still as nature would let him, while the black winds roared down the lanes and alleys that led to the river and threatened to topple him over the low embankment. He was deeply moved by Miss LaSalle's tale; and he was even more moved by her wondrous beauty. He screwed up his face as he thought of avenging his girl by squashing the spidery Mr Janner with a huge cobbler's hammer.

'You shouldn't have had that mutton chop,' said Miss LaSalle, with concern. 'Put your head down between your knees and you'll feel better. Honest, you will . . .'

'It – it's all right,' mumbled Gully. 'Reely.'

'Go on. I won't watch, if you like.'

She turned away and her yellow cloak blew out and smacked Gully in the face. He tottered and sank down till he was able to rest his cold, wet forehead against the cold, wet stones.

'Feeling better, now?'

He opened his eyes and saw Miss LaSalle's worn old shoes shifting in front of him. He stared at them as if with deep interest . . .

'I've had 'em a long time,' she said awkwardly. 'They was my ma's. They used to have pretty buckles . . .'

'I got something,' said Gully impulsively. 'Specially for you.'

He stood up and fumbled in his pocket.

' 'ere,' he said. 'They got Ds on 'em. D for Daisy.'

He brought out the little parcel containing the pinch-beck and brilliant buckles and tore it open.

'Oh! Oh! You shouldn't!' cried Miss LaSalle. 'You shouldn't spend your money like that!'

'Don't you like 'em?'

'Oh yes, yes! They're beautiful! They ain't gold, are they?'

'They're for you,' said Gully, declining to commit himself.

'I could wear them as brooches,' said Miss LaSalle, crying and wiping her eyes on her cloak. 'It seems a shame to put 'em on me shoes where nobody can see 'em.'

'Yes,' agreed Gully. 'In our line, we don't go much on feet.'

'I'll wear them tomorrow!'

'Tomorrer?' repeated Gully with the vague chill of half remembering something.

'When – when we go to see your ma,' went on Miss LaSalle, breathing rapidly and holding on to her young man's arm with a fierce, despairing grip.

Gully stared at her in terror.

'It's all right, ain't it? I can come?' pleaded Miss LaSalle, her voice trembling. 'It's just that I was wondering, hoping you could ask your ma if – if she'd let me work for her . . . in the leather line. I'm very good with me hands, and everyone says I'm quick to learn. I did a bit of leather stitching before I went into the spinning line. Only – only you see, after tonight, I got nowhere to live. So I thought, seeing how your ma is in a big way, she'd give me a chance?'

Before he could answer, she leaned over and kissed him on the cheek.

'Light you 'ome, young lovers?' came the sudden cry of a link-boy as he loitered past. Gully turned, his eyes streaming from the torch's smoke. The flame and the lamplighter's daughter seemed to be composed of the same destructive substance.

' 'ome?' he mumbled, shaking his head. ' 'ome?'

'I won't be no trouble,' said Miss LaSalle anxiously. 'Really I won't. I'll do whatever you say and I won't put a foot wrong.'

'Feet!' groaned Gully, thinking of the shame that gnawed at his soul. 'Christ! All them . . . feet and – and 'IM.'

That night, after he'd got back to Mr Noades's and sprawled somehow onto his bed under the counter, Gully had a horrible dream. He dreamed that he'd given away the buckles he'd bought for Mothering Sunday and that he was going to take Miss LaSalle to the evil-smelling cobbler's shop in Labour-in-Vain Yard. Furthermore he dreamed that he was actually walking along Shoemakers Row with her on his arm and that he was stark naked.

He awoke with a terrible cry and it was morning and he was safe in his bed and not on the open street at all. For a moment he felt a great flood of relief . . . and then he remembered that the nightmare lay, not behind him but ahead. True; he wouldn't be walking down Shoe-makers Row stark naked, but there were worse things than that. The nakedness of the spirit was more shame-ful by far than the nakedness of the body. The thought of the exposure that lay ahead caused him to shrink into his bedclothes and wish he'd never been born.

All that morning he prayed with all his might that Miss LaSalle wouldn't come, that she'd forgotten or that some accident would prevent her. But it was no use. At three o'clock in the afternoon she was waiting outside for him, her yellow cloak flapping and her eyes bright with hope.

'Look,' she said. 'I'm wearing your present!' She lifted up her skirts and displayed her feet, explaining that the buckles had been too heavy for her dress and had dragged it down. 'So I put them on me shoes,' she went on, 'and shortened me skirt so's everyone can see.'

Gully, who was always embarrassed by the sight of feet, turned away and entertained the pathetic hope that Miss LaSalle hadn't meant what she'd said about losing her place and wanting to ask his ma for work. But she had meant it; in fact she'd brought all her posses-sions done up in a neat bundle of brown paper, in-scribed 'Janner. Trig Lane.'

'I'd nowhere to leave it,' she said, and squeezed Gully's arm till he felt his fingers would drop off.

'We'd best go along Carter Lane,' he said, taking the bundle as if he wanted a visible burden to balance the unseen one that was crushing him down. He felt cold, and lonely and frightened.

His friend, the clockmaker's apprentice, who was leaning against the shutters of his master's shop, waved and whistled as Gully and his girl passed by.

'Have a good supper?' he called out. Gully managed a feeble snarl.

'Oh my!' said the clockmaker's apprentice, with exaggerated deference. 'We mustn't talk to common prentices now we're going a-mothering!'

Gully's face grew white . . .

'I suppose I should have brought some flowers or cakes for your ma,' murmured Miss LaSalle apologetically. 'But I put on some scent specially.' She skipped round the other side, for the bundle had come between them. 'D'you like it?'

She put her head close to his: she smelled sweet and warm – like burnt sugar. Gully thought of the foul-smelling shop towards which they were walking, as straight as the flight of a crow. Hastily he turned off Carter Lane and, in an extraordinary mood of cunning and desperation, began to lead his girl through a maze of irrelevant little streets. He was hoping that, either they'd lose themselves and not arrive at all, or that she'd be muddled into thinking that the distance between Shoemakers Row and Labour-in-Vain Yard was really terrific.

'Why, we're almost in Trig Lane!' exclaimed Miss LaSalle in surprise. 'You never said your ma lived so close!'

————≪≪≪≪≪❋≫≫≫≫≫≫——•

Labour-in-Vain gaped in front of them; it was a melancholy pocket off Fish Hill, stuffed full of rubbish by the wild March winds and dirty passers by.

'It's reely,' said Gully defensively, 'quite fashionable when the wind don't blow.'

He paused, as if giving Miss LaSalle a chance to change her mind and escape.

'Shall I take me bundle now?' she asked. 'Your ma won't think it nice, your carrying it.'

He shook his head and he and his girl advanced timidly towards the cobbler's shop. It looked meaner and more wretched than ever as it crouched down between its grimy neighbours as if they'd been beating it. And there was no mistaking it, either: GULLY was painted in large, uneven letters across the parlour window.

'It goes back a long way,' said Gully hopelessly, 'be'ind. You'd be amazed 'ow spayshus it reely is . . . inside.'

'Fancy having your name painted up like that!' said Miss LaSalle; and Gully couldn't help feeling gratified by the sigh she gave. He glanced at her quickly. Sunlight, finding its way somehow into the Yard, seemed to be setting her red hair on fire. For a moment one pride gave way to another as Gully stood and admired his girl; then the door of the cobbler's shop opened and his ma was revealed.

'Why it's Gully!' she said loudly. 'And *walkin'* in all this blowy wind! Why didn't you come by 'ackney carridge, dear?'

'She's got a visitor!' thought Gully with a rush of relief. 'That means the workroom'll be shut and 'E won't be about! So we'll all be able to be'ave natcheral.'

He gazed at his ma approvingly. She'd done herself up quite grandly, with a great deal of embroidery and white edging; and she was wearing a smart little black cap she'd run up out of the silk hatband Gully had given her. In a way she reminded him of old Mrs Noades's funeral cake . . .

His eyes lingered on his ma's, and a mysterious flicker of understanding passed between them as if each was admitting to a loving conspiracy . . . Then Mrs Gully's eyes fixed themselves upon her son's female companion.

'This is Miss LaSalle, ma,' he said. 'She's in the silk an' silver line, y'know.'

'Come inside,' smiled Mrs Gully. 'I got company.'

He saw at once that the workroom door was shut as tight as if it had been nailed and that there was not a boot nor a shoe nor anything to do with feet to be seen anywhere in the parlour. Even the visitor, who sat creaking in a corner chair that was closely guarded by the table, seemed to end up in nothing . . .

'This is Mrs Joker,' said Mrs Gully.

'With a A,' said the new neighbour, creaking forward as much as the furniture allowed. 'Joaker with a A.'

She was an anxious, respectable-looking soul, with black beads and a battered silver brooch.

'Mrs Joaker used to live in 'anover Square.'

'Just orf it, reely . . .'

'You don't say. This is Miss LaSalle.'

'French?' inquired Mrs Joaker, learnedly.

' 'er ma was a 'uge knot,' said Gully, smiling proudly at his ma.

Mrs Gully nodded. 'Reely? I suppose 'er pa must 'ave been in a big way, too?'

'In the oil an' ladder business,' said Gully, avoiding the bright eyes of the lamplighter's daughter.

'Is that so? Mrs Joaker 'ere was tellin' me that she knew someone in the diamond line . . .'

'Well, only in a manner of speakin',' said Mrs Joaker awkwardly, and scraped her chair back against the wall.

'Of course, Miss LaSalle 'ere is in silver. That's right, I believe?'

'Oh yes, ma'am!' said Miss LaSalle, eager to be obliging and on a level with the company. 'Look!' She held out her hands to show the thin black lines that marked her palms and were from the constant passage of the noble metal.

Mrs Joaker inspected them with interest.

'That lady I was tellin' you of, yesterday, Mrs G., used to wash 'er silver in winnygar.'

'We – that is, Mr Janner, always uses 'monia. But it makes you cry like anything.'

'My son,' interposed Mrs Gully, feeling that the two outsiders had conversed sufficiently between themselves, 'won't never bring me silver, just on account of that. The blackenin', you know. It reely 'as to be gold. 'e won't stand for nothing less. Ain't that so, Gully?'

Gully agreed. The feeling in the little parlour was remarkably pleasant. He smiled gratefully at his ma, and once again the secret flicker passed between them.

'Gully never stints me,' she said. 'And why should 'e, bein' in the line 'e is?'

Gully nodded earnestly. He was feeling cheerful and airy, almost as if he was dancing on a web. Everything was turning out far better than he'd hoped; even the sun was coming into the parlour as if it had been invited. It shone respectably through the sign-painted window and wrote GULLY in long letters across the bread-and-butter laden table and fixed a cake with a cherry on it in the black fork of the Y.

Gully chattered on about the grandeur of the Noades's funeral and then about his visit to Janner's, who, as everyone knew, were big in the gold and silver line . . . He stole a glance at his girl; she shifted and blazed up suddenly in the sunlight. He felt momentarily uncomfortable and paused.

'Them's pretty buckles you're wearin', miss,' said Mrs Joaker who had been creaking sideways in her chair as if searching for some way, however unlikely, into the conversation.

'Gully give them to me,' said Miss LaSalle proudly, and held up her feet as high as she could. 'Look! They're Ds. That's for Daisy. It's me name.'

Gully's discomfort increased. Something he'd pushed to the back of his mind, nudged its way forward.

'That lady I was tellin' you of,' went on Mrs Joaker eagerly, 'was called after a flower, too. Marguerite . . .'

'My son's always buyin' presents,' said Mrs Gully, silencing the new neighbour with a look. 'Expense 'as never been a object with Gully, 'as it, dear?'

She glanced coolly at Miss LaSalle's exposed feet and then to the floor beside her son.

'Wh— what was that, ma?'

'I said you was always buyin' presents.'

Gully grew red. He had remembered what he'd tried

to forget; and his ma had remembered, too. It was Mothering Sunday. After all his resolutions, he'd come empty-handed and betrayed his ma and shamed her before Mrs Joaker . . .

Mrs Gully smiled encouragingly at her son. He avoided her eyes and stared bleakly at the floor.

'Ah!' said Mrs Gully, rising and coming towards him with a rattle of disturbed cups. 'Did you think I'd forgot? Dear Gully! Look at 'im, blushin' all over 'is face!' She kissed the air affectionately about an inch above his head. 'Tried to 'ide it from me, didn't you? Wanted me to think you'd forgot! But I saw it! I saw it as soon as you come in, dear . . . your present for Motherin' Sunday! My son,' she said, turning to Mrs Joaker, 'never forgets them old customs. I wonder what 'e's brung me this time?'

'Ma!' cried Gully in sudden terror; but he was too late. Mrs Gully had bent down and taken, from the floor beside him, the neat little bundle of Miss LaSalle's possessions!

Gully saw his girl's hand reach out – then vanish like

a flame extinguished. A sensation of fearful cold engulfed him and he began to shiver violently. He thought he was going to have a seizure.

'The lady I was tellin' you of,' said Mrs Joaker, eyeing the bundle with painful curiosity, 'used to get buttons. Real pearl buttons. One every year . . .'

'Buttons?' murmured Mrs Gully, admiring the bundle before clearing a place and depositing it in the middle of the table. 'Fancy that!'

'But then,' said Mrs Joaker, twisting and turning in her chair in order to examine the bundle from all sides, 'she 'ad almost everything else. And buttons always comes in 'andy.'

Gully and his girl sat in terror and stared at the bundle as if it was a severed head.

'Janner. Trig Lane,' mouthed Gully, reading the inscription on the brown paper. For a moment he entertained the forlorn hope that the bundle might contain a quantity of nicked silver; but the glimpses he kept catching of Miss LaSalle showed a different sort of fear from guilt. In a strange way he felt she was frightened, not *of* his ma, but *for* her.

'Shall I open it now, or after tea, dear?'

'It – it—' began to plead Miss LaSalle, when suddenly the little parlour shook as in an earthquake and the tea-things jumped in agitation.

A loud, insistent hammering had begun from behind the closed door of the workroom. In Gully's ears, it sounded as grim and threatening as the fist of the angel of doom.

'It's 'IM,' said Mrs Gully, nodding towards the thin partition that divided the workroom from the parlour. ' 'E wants 'IS tea.'

She never referred to her journeyman by name, but always as HE or HIM, and in tones of sombre mystery.

The hammering ceased and a silence fell upon the parlour. Everyone stared uncomfortably towards the closed door. Gully felt as if he was really going to faint. He put out his hands to hold on to the table. Already, in his mind's eye, he could see the workroom door opening and the dark, brutish place within being exposed. He could see the ugly, ancient man who lurked there, spitting on his hands and, as usual, missing them and spattering his knees and the floor . . . the old, old man with his rheumy eyes, his boiled nose and his hideous bunioned feet. Already the stink was in his nostrils . . .

'I'd ha' thought,' he whispered miserably, 'that it bein' Sunday—'

'You know what 'E is,' said Mrs Gully malevolently. 'But this time 'E'll 'ave to wait!' She shouted out this last sentiment loudly enough for the journeyman to hear. 'E'll 'ave to wait till we've 'ad our tea and I've opened me present what Gully's brung me for Motherin' Sunday!'

She was answered by two bangs, denoting either impatience or assent.

She ignored them and began, with elaborate courtesy, to offer round tea and cake. But no one – not even Mrs Joaker – had any appetite. As usual, HE had spoiled things and it was impossible for the conversation to return to its previous refined level; not with HIM grunting and shifting and banging about next door!

There was no help for it but to do without tea and take everybody's mind off HIM by opening up the present Gully had brought. Mrs Gully stood up and cleared a space round the bundle.

'It's all right, dear,' she said, as Miss LaSalle stretched out a trembling hand. 'I can manage the knot meself.'

'They used to come in little velvet boxes,' said Mrs Joaker, dragging her chair until she was pressed tightly against the table.

'What did?'

'Them pearls I was tellin' you of.'

'Oh, them buttons.'

'Well, they 'ad to be buttons, seein' as 'ow she 'ad a pearl necklace what was give 'er by the gentleman.'

'One button a year don't seem much for a mother to get,' said Mrs Gully, loosening the knot that secured the bundle. 'At that rate she'd be in 'er grave before she 'ad any use of 'em. My Gully's got a bit more pride than to bring 'is mother . . .'

She pulled away the cord and let it fall. Miss LaSalle bent to pick it up – and remained half under the table. Gully could see her red hair smouldering near his feet.

'It's well done up,' said Mrs Gully, delicately lifting up a torn shift and shaking it. 'Whatever can it be, Gully dear?'

She pulled out a filthy petticoat; Miss LaSalle's dismissal had been too sudden for her to have time to wash her belongings before packing them.

'Where is it, Gully?' asked his ma, coming upon a pair of stockings that were as thick with grime as they were thin with holes. She held them up and shook them in a puzzled kind of way, as if her gift might have been caught up in them. A singularly stale smell spread across the table.

She found a bodice, frayed and stained with grease, and then other items of such humble and pitiful an aspect that no one should have seen them, let alone held them up to a neighbour's fascinated view.

'They – they're mine!' sobbed Miss LaSalle, lifting her face to the level of the table so that Gully saw it was shining with tears of shame.

'Reely?'

Mrs Gully had begun to gather the articles together. Blindly she included a plate . . .

'Ma!' moaned Gully.

'Yes?' said Mrs Gully, as if surprised that anyone in the present company should address her so familiarly.

She had completed her packing up, and was now grasping the bundle with hands in which the veins and sinews stood out like seams in leather.

'Get out of 'ere,' she said quietly. 'Get out.'

Then, with a movement so unexpected in its rapidity, that Gully had no chance to defend himself, she flung the bundle in her son's face.

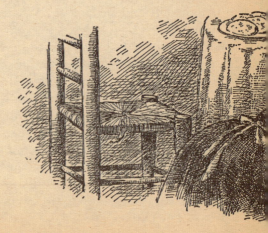

'Get out!' she screamed. 'Get out – get out of my
'ouse!'

Gully, half blinded by his girl's ramshackle belongings, made a stupid, clumsy effort to save the plate.

'But ma—'

'Don't you dare to call me ma!' shrieked Mrs Gully,
her fists clenched and her eyes blazing. 'You proud little
wiper, you!'

'But me—'

'Look at 'im standin' there!' raged Mrs Gully, and
then, heedless of the onlookers, began to call upon the

ceiling, it seemed, to witness the scorn and disgust, the vile ingratitude and even the hatred that she saw, like running sores, in her son's eyes.

Gully shrank back as his ma's words poured over him like a burning torrent. He actually felt them scald and sting. Fearfully he raised his hand . . . 'For Gawd's sake, ma—'

'What do you know about Gawd? Motherin' Sunday, is it? More like Murderin' Sunday! Look at 'im, I say, standin' there with 'is fancy girl! And 'er as filthy as a rubbish 'eap!'

Gully saw his girl shudder and her face twist up in pain.

'Shut your mouth!' he shouted. 'Shut your 'orrible mouth!'

'Gully – Gully . . . please!' moaned Miss LaSalle, swaying like a flame about to go out.

'I told you, I ain't your ma no more!'

'Then good riddance!'

'I 'ate you for your snaky pride!'

'And I 'ate you for everythin' else! I 'ate this place and I 'ate this Yard—'

'Labour-in-Vain Yard!' screamed out Mrs Gully in terrible triumph. 'And labour in vain it was to bring you into the world!'

'And labour in vain it's been to live in it!' howled Gully, and smashed down the plate he'd still been holding.

Then the sky fell down – or so it seemed. There came a violent crash from the workroom that shook the whole house! It was followed by a sharp grunt of pain.

'It's 'IM,' muttered Mrs Gully, recovering herself a little and panting heavily.

'What's 'E done now?'

'Knocked something over. Just like 'IM.'

There came now from the workroom a moan of intolerable agony.

'Christ!' said Gully. ' 'E's 'urt 'IMSELF.'

'I'll go—' began Gully's girl, for neither the mother nor the son seemed able to move.

Gully stared at her in bewilderment, then he turned back to his ma. The look that passed between them was stripped of all its secrecy now. Together they rushed to the workroom door.

'Can't do nothing right, can 'E!' cried Mrs Gully.

'And on a Sunday, too!' sobbed Gully, dragging open the door so wildly that the thin partition shook like the walls of Jericho.

The old familiar smell came rushing out and engulfed the parlour like a great warm garment. Gully and his ma went into the dark room where a single candle burned on the cobbler's bench, and cast a subdued radiance on the racks of worn tools.

Shadowy boots crowded the shelves round the walls, and a beggars' host of them stood patiently in a corner of the floor, as if listening to a sermon. Wrinkled and broken, they reeked mournfully, with their uppers displaying every deformity of leather, reflecting the ways in which men and women walked the world. The cobbler's workroom was like a dim graveyard of feet, awaiting the resurrection of soles.

The old man himself was lying on the floor and crying with pain. Somehow the heavy cobbler's last had fallen over and crushed his naked, bunioned foot.

' 'E must 'ave done it 'IMSELF!' wept Gully, and knelt beside the old journeyman.

'Pull it off – pull it off!' urged Mrs Gully, crouching beside her son and holding on to his sleeve.

Very gently, Gully lifted up the last and his ma moved the candle to examine the injured foot. It was a frightful bruised and bloody sight; the toes had been crushed and the old man moaned and moaned.

'Bring some warm water!' called out Mrs Gully. 'From the tea.'

Miss LaSalle ran to fetch the jug and the cleanest rag from among her scattered belongings. Gully took them and, with great care and tenderness, began to wash the blood from the old man's foot.

'Thank you . . . thank you,' he mumbled, and, looking up at Gully's girl, smiled painfully. 'And you too, miss.'

'Do it – do it 'urt much?' asked Mrs Gully, nervously patting the old man's hand.

'Not too bad . . . not now you're all 'ere.'

' 'ow did it 'appen?'

'I got frightened with all that shoutin'. And then I 'eard a plate breakin' . . .'

'It weren't nothing, reely. It weren't anything worth menshunning.'

'Reely?'

'On me honour. Ain't that so, Gully, dear?'

Mrs Gully looked at her son. They both nodded earnestly and smiled. The old man seemed reassured.

'I like what 'e brung you for this Motherin' Sunday,' he mumbled, twisting his head and peering about him.

'Oh that,' said Mrs Gully uncomfortably. 'It weren't nothing, reely.'

'Oh, but it were!' He was looking now at Gully's girl and his watery eyes were blinking as if before too bright a light. 'I never see'd a present so pretty. And French, too. You made a good choice, Gully. Your ma and me is reely proud!'

'It – it's me pa,' said Gully softly, as if his words might have blown out the candle. 'Miss LaSalle, this 'ere is Mr Gully. Me pa.'

As he spoke, a limitless happiness suddenly flooded Gully's soul. The weight he'd lifted from his father's foot was as thistledown beside the weight he'd lifted from himself. He wanted to dance and sing; he wanted to rush out into Labour-in-Vain Yard and shout his good news to the sun and sky. He wanted to embrace and kiss everyone, even perfect strangers who might be passing up and down Fish Hill!

But he had to content himself with reaching out for

Miss LaSalle's hand and explaining, 'Me pa, 'ere, mends soles, y'know. We're only in a small way, but we're a 'appy little family reely.'

He felt his girl's grip answer his own and squeeze and squeeze till it seemed she'd never let go. Then Mrs Joaker managed to edge her way into the room and the candle flame flickered so that all the boots and shoes seemed to dance for the old cobbler with his wife and son.

'I'd best bandage up 'IS foot,' said Mrs Gully with a touch of her old gentility. 'It do look a ugly mess!'

'Oh no!' put in Mrs Joaker, who had been pew-opener at the church in Hanover Square. ' *'ow beautiful are the feet of them that preach the gospel of peace*!'

The old cobbler nodded and smiled with rare contentment . . .